No Use Pretending

Iowa Short Fiction Award

No Use Pretending

Stories

Thomas A. Dodson

University of Iowa Press · Iowa City

University of Iowa Press, Iowa City 52242
Copyright © 2023 by Thomas A. Dodson
uipress.uiowa.edu
Printed in the United States of America

Cover design by TG Design
Text design and typesetting by Sara T. Sauers
Printed on acid-free paper

Library of Congress Cataloging-in-Publication Data
Names: Dodson, Thomas A., 1976– author.
Title: No Use Pretending: Stories / Thomas A. Dodson.
Description: Iowa City: University of Iowa Press, [2023]. |
    Series: Iowa Short Fiction Award
Identifiers: LCCN 2023001499 (print) |
    LCCN 2023001500 (ebook) |
    ISBN 9781609389178 (paperback) |
    ISBN 9781609389185 (ebook)
Subjects: LCGFT: Short stories.
Classification: LCC PS3604.O3325 N68 2023 (print) |
    LCC PS3604.O3325 (ebook) |
    DDC 813/.6—dc23/eng/20230209
LC record available at https://lccn.loc.gov/2023001499
LC ebook record available at https://lccn.loc.gov/2023001500

Contents

No Use Pretending

Keeping

IT WAS A HUMBLING thing, asking for help like this, needing it so badly. But removing his hat, brushing flakes of snow from brim and crown, Guy knew there was no other way. His neighbors' fields, already stripped of corn and soybeans, would soon be a single plain of snow, patches of winter rye the only green for acres. Cold winds would blow freely across all that flatness, gathering strength until they reached the stand of pines at the edge of his apiary. The trees would provide a break, and he could wrap the hives in tar paper to keep out the frost, but it wouldn't be enough. His bees, what was left of them, they wouldn't survive an Iowa winter. He needed to take them west.

He'd been standing on the porch of Taylor's place, weighed down with what he meant to ask, when he heard the baby crying. It wailed and wailed, a helpless thing, full to the top with need. When it hushed, he opened the screen and knocked. Taylor's wife answered. She had the baby with her, his head covered in wisps of fine brown hair, face pressed to her breast, sucking away. Guy coughed and looked down at his shoes.

"Come in," Andrea said, unconcerned. "Taylor's out back, finishing up."

He followed her inside, ducking to avoid the transom. Forty-odd years lifting supers filled with honey, each box heavy as a newborn calf, had stooped his shoulders. But all told, work in the beeyard had done him good. He hadn't dwindled like other men his age, was still broad-backed and tall. He knew to move carefully in these old farmhouses.

In the dining room, his eyes were drawn to the glass-windowed cabinet. Built to house pickled beets and jars of homemade jam, Taylor's wife had stocked it with books, their spines emblazoned with words like "feminist," "gay and lesbian," "queer." He could remember a time when it would have been dangerous to have such books where people could see them. "Ain't much difference," his father had said, "between a cocksucker and a communist."

"You're in your Sunday best," Andrea said. "Business in town?" She lowered herself into a chair and settled the baby on her lap.

"The bank. Every once in a while they like to bring you in, turn you upside down, see if anything falls out." She smiled politely. In truth, it was only for this visit that he'd traded his work boots for Oxfords, set aside his overalls, and retrieved his suit from the back of the closet. He'd worn it last ten years ago, at Alma's funeral.

The backdoor clattered shut, and Taylor called from the kitchen. "Something got at one of the hives. Scat on the ground and some bees chewed and spat out."

"In here," Andrea said. "Guy stopped by."

"Oh yeah?" Taylor said cheerfully. She strode into the room, wiping her hands on the front of her jeans, the cuffs still tucked into her socks. She placed a hand on Andrea's shoulder, bent down and kissed the baby's head. The chair next to Andrea was stacked with papers. Taylor cleared them and sat down.

"Should've phoned first," Guy said, shifting in his seat.

"You're always welcome, you know that." The tips of his ears burning, he looked at his hands. These bouts of bashfulness, they sometimes happened around Taylor. She was just so—he couldn't think of a better word for it—handsome. She reminded him of James Dean in *East of Eden*, and also, vaguely, of Milton Law, a high school classmate and the first boy he'd ever kissed.

"Brought you this." Setting his hat on the table, he retrieved the package from under his arm, a square section of honeycomb in a clear plastic box. He'd selected, for his offering, a product of his strongest hive. Workers had filled each of the cells with amber honey, sealed them over with the freshest wax. It was a beautiful comb, white-capped and neatly cut. Something to be proud of.

"You didn't have to do that," Andrea said. "You know, Taylor keeps trying to win me over to the dark stuff." Her face crinkled and she shook her head from side to side. "It's not for me, though. Too funky."

"I've always been too funky for you, *mi reina*."

Taylor had seeded a portion of her land with buckwheat. Bees that fed on its white-petaled flowers made dark honey—near to black—nutty and pleasingly bitter. More traditional, Guy kept his meadows stocked with wildflowers: Shasta daisies and black-eyed Susans, clover that bloomed in shades of white, pink, and crimson. His bees rewarded him with a sweet, light honey he sold to grocery stores, driving in each week to stock the shelves himself.

"You say you've got some critter nosing into a hive?"

"What do you think?" Taylor said. "A raccoon?"

"Skunk more likely. You can put up chicken wire. She'll have to stand up on her hind legs and the bees can sting her belly. Or you could set a trap."

The baby began to fuss and Andrea excused herself. She bundled the boy in a sling and carried him away, her flip-flops slapping as she mounted the stairs. Guy sat across from Taylor in silence. Most of the time, it was easy between them. They'd known each other for going on eight years now, ever since she'd come to the beekeepers' meeting at the VFW hall. She'd had so many questions, been so eager to learn the trade.

He'd invited her to join him in his beeyard, a kind of apprenticeship. Later, when he'd gotten a call from the fire department about a swarm hanging from a picnic table in Happy Hollow Park, they'd gone together to capture it. They'd smoked the bees, doused them with sugar spray, and shook them into one of his spare supers. He'd given her the box and all the bees inside, her first colony. Together they'd cleared her backyard, transformed it into an apiary. She ran her own operation now, small but thriving. That was how their friendship worked, Guy offering help and advice, passing on the craft, taking pride in Taylor's success. But this, asking her for help—real help, the kind that involved sacrifice—it felt wrong.

"Guy, is everything all right? You seem, I don't know, bothered."

"It's been a hard year," he began, "a real hard year."

He told Taylor about the outbreak of nosema. Bees with swollen guts had deposited smears of brown diarrhea down the sides of the supers. They fell from the boxes, littering the ground with their hollowed-out carcasses. Others perished midflight, some bearing fat wads of pollen, food their spore-ravaged stomachs could no longer digest. He'd lost other hives to mites, passed from bee to bee until they reached the brood chamber. There they fed on larva and laid their eggs, fouling whole colonies.

And then there were the bees that ranged beyond his meadow. In August, he'd found a pile of dead bees in front of one of his hives, the rest stumbling around like they were drunk. He couldn't prove it was chemicals killing them, but during the summer months, he'd seen plenty of crop dusters swing low over the nearby fields, raining pesticides down on the corn.

That was as much as he was willing to tell Taylor, or anybody else. The truth, he knew, was that he was to blame for the bees' decline. Autry Honey had been a family business, his wife and sons all chipping in. After the boys went away to college and Alma passed, he'd hired help for processing and bottling, an accountant for the books, seasonal workers whenever he needed an extra hand. But the bees, he cared for them himself, alone.

It had worked out fine for a couple of years. But last summer, not long after his seventy-third birthday, he'd found himself standing in front of a hive, not sure what he was doing there. The cover was off, his smoker spent. Had he set out to harvest honey or check for a sick queen?

Since then, he'd kept his logbook close, looked up things he'd once kept in his head—when and how much he'd fed each colony, whether he'd treated them for pests. And then there was the time he lost the book, wasted a whole afternoon searching. He spotted it the next morning while scrambling eggs over the range. On the shelf by the window, the frayed binding sticking out from a row of Alma's cookbooks.

Pests and chemicals hadn't killed his bees, at least not on their own. Some died every year, but well-tended colonies could bounce back. He owed his losses to sloppy stewardship, enough to put his whole operation at risk. He'd failed his charges, left them vulnerable.

"I treated the hives for mites and all," he explained. "Had to torch the sickest ones. All told, I'm down to one-third what I should have this time of year. Not enough to make the contract out west; colonies too weak to winter up here."

"Jesus," Taylor said, leaning back in her chair. "If I'd have known, maybe we could have. . . . So, what are you going to do? Get them indoors, a barn or something? Then buy nucs in the spring?"

Guy chuckled bitterly. "With what money? And besides, I can't wait for the thaw. First winter storm, and I'll be finished." He couldn't bring himself to look Taylor in the eyes, so he looked instead into the kitchen, at the high chair and the sink full of dishes. "I can see you've got your hands full here. And I hate to ask, but . . . "

"Hey, Guy, whatever you need." Taylor reached across the table. Forgetting himself, he gripped her fingers. There was no sorting out everything he felt—humiliation, gratitude, a shameful urge to seize and cling to this sudden closeness between them, for it to mean something it didn't. He released her hand and straightened up in his chair. He was a foolish old man.

"All the bees I have left, they're healthy. You've got my word."

Her lips slightly parted, Taylor waited for him to explain.

"The California trip," he said, "the almond bloom. It's good money. Real good money." He retrieved his notes from the breast pocket of his suit, unfolded them, and set them in front of her. "Now inspections, truck rental, equipment—that's all settled." He tapped twice on the top page, where he'd written out all the expenses. "That comes out of my end. The profit, though, we split fifty-fifty. I've got a Class A license, had it for years, so I'll do the driving."

"Guy, what are we talking about, exactly?"

"I leave in three weeks, but I don't have the hives. Not enough, anyway. I need your bees, together with mine. I'm sorry to come asking, but I need you to come with me to California."

A rumble strip throbbed beneath his feet, and Guy nudged the truck away from the shoulder. The wind was up, and he had to keep a firm grip on the wheel. The sky was a monolith of low gray clouds, spitting needles of sleet against the windshield.

In spite of the weather, things had gone easy. He'd managed to keep his cool when tailgaters blew their horns, to swing the trailer into traffic as they passed through Des Moines and Omaha. Taking charge of a twenty-ton rig, sending it hurtling down I-80, it might have intimidated another man. But back in Vietnam he'd been the driver for a Patton tank, crashing through the jungle, taking point on thunder runs: top speed with one track on the asphalt, the other spraying mud, all guns firing, praying they didn't hit a mine. And anyway, he'd made this trip before, every year for the past five, and always on his own.

That morning he'd found Taylor on her porch, slumped in a rocking chair. It was before dawn, and the house was dark. He hadn't asked if Andrea would be seeing them off. The stars were veiled, and a rabbit flung itself into the dark as he turned his headlights to the beeyard. He helped Taylor load her hives onto the flatbed, next to his own. When they were ready to leave, he offered her the little mattress behind the driver's seat—he'd raised children too, knew how hard it was to get a decent night's sleep with a baby in the house. Taylor said no, promised through yawns to help navigate.

Hours later, and she was still out cold, strapped into the passenger seat, her temple pressed against the glass of the cab. There was a sign for gas and he took the exit for the travel plaza. Taylor stirred and looked around.

"Everything okay back there?" she said, putting a hand through her dark, upswept hair.

"Sure. They're strapped in tight. We had some weather, but that's what the tarps are for."

Taylor looked once over her shoulder, then drew a phone from her chore coat. Splashing sounds came from the speaker, then a woman's voice, a rhythmic murmuring, together with a child's happy clamor.

"Andrea sent a video," she said. "Oscar in the tub." The warmth that spread over her face, it had nothing to do with Guy, but watching it made him feel close to her. The brakes hissed, then sighed as he eased the rig alongside a bank of diesel pumps. She tapped briefly on the screen, then pocketed the phone.

"The tank's on my side, I'll fill her up."

"All right," he said. "I think I'll stretch my legs."

"Do you know how to work that thing or what?" said the man in line behind him. Guy was staring down at the card reader, his fingers hovering over the keypad. Had he already paid for the gas?

"Your card's run," the cashier was saying, "just need your PIN." Place like this, no reason to think they would cheat you. Best to play along. But looking down at the blank place on the screen, he couldn't conceive of what numbers ought to go there. He had to put in something, but if the numbers were wrong, they'd make him start all over.

"Step aside, some of us have loads to haul."

"Just a minute," Guy grumbled.

Alma. The number had to do with her, but how? And where was she, anyway? Still in the bathroom? Every damn time. And if it wasn't her, it was one of the boys. Couldn't get more than sixty miles without having to pull off somewhere.

But no, that was a different time. Years ago. He was here with Taylor now. The card. The machine. She needed him to pay for the gas. He glanced over at a display rack. Did they have that gum he liked? The kind that tasted like licorice?

"Hey, I'm talking to you." Someone tapped him on the shoulder. A trucker. He seemed to be grinding his teeth, the muscles along his jaw visibly taut. One of his arms was badly sunburnt, the pale underflesh fringed with translucent patches of dead skin like a molting reptile.

"Quiet, now." Guy turned back to the machine, waving his hand in the air as if swatting an insect. The next thing he knew, Taylor was there, saying his name.

Sneering, the trucker turned to Taylor, sized her up. "And whose going to make me? You? Your little boyfriend here?" He looked both exhausted and agitated. Kept awake by chemicals, capable of anything. The cashier, secure behind her bullet-resistant window, watched warily but said nothing.

"Fifty on pump nine," Taylor said, shoving a wad of bills into the metal drawer beneath the window. "Happy now, asshole? Guy, take your card, we need to go."

When they got back to the rig, Taylor reached under her seat. She unzipped her nylon bag, packed with snacks and other essentials, and drew out a handgun, trigger and barrel secured in a molded-plastic holster. "You okay to drive?" she asked, arching her back and tucking the pistol into the waistband of her jeans.

"I'm fine," he said, not sure yet if he was. He started the engine.

"Let's go, then. I don't want that psycho following us."

"Her birthday," Guy said when they were back on the interstate.

"What?"

"The PIN. Five four forty-eight." Alma's birthday. How could he have forgotten a thing like that?

It wasn't until hours later, when they'd traded the foothills of Arkansas for the Colorado Rockies, that Taylor stopped checking the rearview mirror, peering into the cab of every semi that got too close. Later, they pulled into a Safeway parking lot in Grand Junction, as good a place as any to spend the night. Guy insisted Taylor take the sleeper cab. "My truck," he said when she protested, "my rules. And that gun, we need to talk about that, too. Can I have a look?"

Taylor considered, then took the pistol out of its holster and handed it over. "I guess I should have said something about it."

"Probably," he said, checking the safety was on. An all-metal, hammer-fired semiautomatic; a newer model, but not so different from the Colt 1911 he'd carried in Vietnam. "This size, I'd think it would be chambered for forty-five caliber. But it's light."

"It's a twenty-two. I take it with me when I go camping."

"We're pretty far from the woods," he said, handing it back.

"Don't tell Andrea, all right? She doesn't understand about guns."

"I guess it's your own business."

"It is," Taylor said. "Two thousand miles, to somewhere I don't know anybody, where truckers and farmers and drunks—any man, basically—can decide he doesn't like my clothes, or my walk.... I know what they're like, what they do. No way I'm ranging cross-country and leaving my gun at home."

It occurred to him that his idea of Taylor's life might be distorted: his notion that she'd had it easier, never knowing a world that expected her to hide—at least not the way he had. But refusing to hide, even now, no doubt there were risks to that, too. Things he knew nothing about.

"Well, all right," he said, forcing a grin. "So long as you don't point it at me."

When Taylor was settled, Guy folded himself into a sort of crouch in the passenger seat. Feet propped on the dash, he tried to quiet his mind. The incident at the truck stop had left him shaken. The way he'd fallen out of the world, it was like slipping on black ice. No warning, no chance to catch himself. And that trucker running his mouth, as if Guy was nothing at all. The worst of it had been Taylor standing there, a witness to his infirmity. He'd tried to apologize, but she'd just shrugged. No big deal, she'd said. She forgot things, too: passwords, birthdays, the names of Andrea's nieces. If she suspected there was something he wasn't telling her, she seemed willing to let it go.

No point going into it anyway. He needed only to stay vigilant, focus on the tasks in front of him. A few weeks was all, and then he'd be back home with his bees. He'd kept bigger secrets than this from neighbors and friends—from his children—and for much longer.

The next morning, he took a handful of Advil to soothe the pain in his back, and they traversed the whole of Utah. A sheen of still water stood over the salt flats, an enormous mirror perfectly reflecting mountains and clouds. I-80 was a bridge that split the sky.

Just before nightfall, they took the on-ramp to the Vegas Freeway. The Trump Hotel was visible for miles, a tower of gold-infused glass, tarnished by the late afternoon sun. They pushed on to the San Joaquin Valley, then checked into a motel outside Bakersfield. When they got to the room, they each claimed a bed and fell asleep in their clothes.

After a breakfast of coffee, eggs, and chicken fried steak, they set out for the Singh family orchard. Guy turned off the highway and on to a rutted access road. Beyond a rail wood fence stood rows of short, sturdy almond trees, an occasional pink-white blossom ornamenting their branches. When they reached the fence line, Taylor climbed down from the cab and swung open the cattle gate.

It was hours unloading, setting the hives on pallets at the end of each row of trees, Guy's arrayed nearer to the gate so he wouldn't have to walk as far to tend them. Their hives looked more or less the same, handmade boxes he'd shown Taylor how to craft from wood and wire. Still easy enough to tell apart. For years, it had been his practice, after assembling each box, to brand it with a home-crafted iron, an *AH* for Autry Honey, the rough letters encircled by a crooked oval.

When they were finished, they sat with their backs against the trunks, in the shade of the new-blooming boughs. The sun was high in the sky, and across the row, Taylor was gulping water from a plastic bottle. She'd shed her shirt, and in her tank top he could see her shapely shoulders and the hard, lean muscles of her arms. It wasn't ogling, he told himself. It had never been her woman's body that fascinated him, but something to do with her gestures, her walk, the mix of confidence and vulnerability. His attraction to her was nothing like what he'd felt for Alma: great love but wan desire. It was more like what he felt for other men.

He wondered if there might be a kind of manliness that didn't belong to men at all, one possessed instead only by certain kinds of women: the butch lesbians he'd seen in bars in the city, a few women he'd known in the service, the girl in his town who'd stayed a tomboy even into high school, so bold as to take a boy's name—before her parents sent her away. These women, gay or straight, he'd felt they were like him somehow.

Did Taylor excite him, or did he envy her, the kind of freedom she had, a self-assurance he'd always wanted but had never been able to inhabit? He looked at his boots, determined not to think about her anymore. Whatever these feeling were, they had to be wrong. It had been this way since he was a boy; he kept wanting the wrong things.

"Ready?" he said, and cleared his throat.

They zipped into their bee suits and lit the smokers. Guy knew keepers who burned wooden pellets, burlap, even cotton waste. Though it meant shouldering a satchel from hive to hive, he'd brought fuel from home: long dry needles from the pines that grew on his land. He loved the smell of smoldering pine straw, the cool, white clouds coiling from the funnel.

He directed a few puffs into the first box, then waited, giving the guards time to abandon their posts and wander, drowsily, deeper into the hive. Outside, bees hovered and dipped, drawing looping lines through the air. Others had begun to investigate the trees, lighting on the few flowers already in bloom.

Occasionally, a bee landed on his bare hands, crawled about, and then departed. He'd stopped wearing gloves years ago. They were bulky, and besides, if you moved slowly and with care, few bees would sting you. Removing the covers and breaking seals of dried resin with his hive tool, he lifted the frames, then searched each box until he found the queen.

He was putting the cover back on a hive when an SUV, freshly waxed and gleaming, pulled into the grove. Taylor was at the far end of the orchard, too far to hear him call. He removed his veil and walked alone in the direction of the gate. The vehicle's windows were tinted, and he couldn't make out the driver until the door swung open. A well-fed man in his thirties, his face framed by a short black beard. Erjot Singh.

Guy had met Erjot's father, the Singh family patriarch, but just the once. The old man had gotten his start as a laborer in other men's orchards, eventually saving enough to buy land of his own. Erjot, the eldest son, managed things now. Guy had heard the workers call him "the Little Prince." He lived lavishly, it was said, and would, on his father's death, inherit the Singh empire: two thousand acres of rich, central valley farmland, almond and pistachio orchards and a vineyard for growing raisin grapes.

The two men shook hands and talked in the language of farmers: weather, soil, seeds. And, because this was California, water. Erjot gestured to a plastic bucket. A line of bees was already marshaled along the rim, others perched on chips of wood that bobbed on the surface.

"We've had drought here the last two years. Micro-irrigation, fly-over imaging—we've got to watch every drop."

"I hear you," Guy said. "But if they're lacking for water on-site, they'll go looking for it. That's time they're not pollinating your trees." Erjot didn't assent, but he didn't argue, either.

They walked along a couple of rows, Guy showing off the hives, Erjot examining his trees.

"You're just in time," Erjot said when they were back at the gate.

"Another day or two and all these trees will be in bloom. Big money," he mused. "Small window."

"Well," Guy said, trying to sound good-humored, "we sure hauled ass to get here."

They shook hands again and Erjot gave him the first payment, a check made out to Autry Honey.

The next day, they slept in and took their time getting ready. He'd wanted to talk to Taylor about how to divide the day's work, but for most of the drive to the orchard, she was on her phone.

"That's not going to happen," she said. "Well, she's my cousin, actually. You're being crazy." She was silent for a long moment, then sighed. "Look, it's just me and Guy, *cariño*. It's all orchards and IHOPS out here. Sweat and dirt and a motel off the interstate. As soon as we're done, as soon as we've made this money, I'll be home again."

"Everything all right?" he asked when she was through.

"She's acting like I'm out here on spring break. And you know how my mom came up, to help with Oscar? I guess she's bossing Andrea around."

At the orchard, he went looking for a hose while Taylor got into her suit; he'd top off the buckets and walk the rows before suiting up, see how his bees were taking to their new diet. He got as far as the first tree before he stopped, confused. Two hives, ones he'd tended himself the day before, had vanished along with their pallets.

He willed himself to concentrate. Surely, he hadn't lost his mind completely.

At his feet, a jumble of symbols had been pressed into the dirt. Gradually, he registered the marks for what they were: indentations left by pallet slats, together with bootprints and the overlapping tracks of forklifts. Almond flowers, both flattened and freshly fallen, lay in the wide chevrons of the tread marks, the pink blossoms smoldering against the dark earth. Shielding his eyes, he looked down the next row and the next. Gone. All of them gone.

He found himself walking, as if in a trance, toward one of the remaining hives. There was a scent in the air—alarm pheromone, a smell like banana taffy. Bees landed on the bare flesh of his neck and arms, stinging. As they pulled free, viscera tore from their abdomens—venom and acid sacks left behind.

"Guy," Taylor called. "Hey, Guy!"

"Who would do this?" he said. And then, for the first time since Alma died, he began to cry.

"These guys, they knew what they were doing," the sheriff said. "How many did you lose?"

Guy leaned against the fence, his face in his hands, unable to speak.

"More than half," he heard Taylor say. "A hundred fifty, maybe? We haven't had a chance to count."

The number didn't matter. There were too few left to fulfill the contract with the Singhs, or even to run his operation back home. Insurance might pay out for an injured worker or a tornado, but not for this. With no money to replenish his stocks, the only asset he had was the apiary itself, the land on which he'd lived and worked for years. In one night, he'd lost everything, and worse, he'd taken Taylor down with him. The shame of his impotence, his selfishness, it was almost more than he could bear.

Back in the motel room, they sat at the end table with the curtains drawn. Taylor had scraped the stingers from his neck and shoulders, pressed dollops of calamine lotion onto her fingertips and dabbed them onto the welts. What he must look like to her. His bare chest, strong but sagging. Tangles of spider veins visible beneath the sagging flesh of his arms. Normally, he would have resisted, embarrassed to be shirtless in front of her. But after what had happened, he was past any care for pride or propriety.

"You can do the rest yourself," she said, tossing the crumpled tube on the table. She paced the length of the room, her boots leaving muddy prints on the thin carpet.

His shirt was hanging over the empty chair, but reaching for it seemed impossible. He'd experienced something like this before, coming back from the war, a week when all he could do was sit, slumped and motionless on the living room couch. Later, Alma had told him that he'd refused to eat or take himself to the bathroom. Whenever she tried to speak to him, he would grimace and turn away.

Their doctor, a family friend, came to the house to examine him, but found nothing wrong. The next day, he returned with release forms for electroconvulsive therapy. Alma had feared their life together was over. But then, one afternoon, as she was eating cottage cheese in the kitchen, he'd sat up and asked for a glass of water. He hadn't had an episode since.

"Motherfuckers!" Taylor shouted, sweeping a lamp off the nightstand, sending it crashing to the floor, the bulb flaring out with a dull pop. Not satisfied, she kicked it across the room. Guy stared at the crumpled shade, crooked on its base, then at Taylor, hands on her hips, practically panting with fury.

"I need you to snap out of it, Guy. I need you to get mad."

His shirt hung over a chair back. He fixed his gaze on it, but when he willed his arm to move, some invisible force held him in place. He closed his eyes and gathered his strength. Like a man walking into a strong wind, he strained his body forward. He reached out and grasped blindly. When he opened his eyes, he had the shirt collar crumpled in his fist. He pulled it over his head.

"Tomorrow," Taylor said. "As soon as the sun is up. We'll get a map. We'll go down every back road, see if they were stupid enough to put them out someplace we can find them."

They spent the next two days driving around in a rented sedan, scanning the deserts and canyons of the San Joaquin Valley for any sign of the hives. It wasn't entirely hopeless; the land on either side of I-50 was flat for hundreds of miles, punctuated occasionally by a gas station, a fast food restaurant, or a field of pumpjacks. There were only so many places to hide the bright white boxes, fewer if the thieves hoped to keep the bees alive and healthy for resale. Besides, what was the alternative?

Locking himself in the motel room with the curtains drawn, pinned to the bed by dread? At least this way, they were doing something.

"What did you say to Andrea?" he said. "That is, if you don't mind my asking."

"I told her the people here are assholes. I told her we're getting sick of each other." Taylor took a hand off the wheel and dug out some sunflower seeds from the bag in her lap. She cracked one open with her teeth and spat the shell out the window.

"And that's all?"

"Just watch your side, okay?"

It was the first words they'd spoken to each other all afternoon.

"I just want to fix this," she said finally. "We fix it, finish the job, and she never has to know." She shifted another seed from her cheek, cracked, and spat again. "You and Alma. You had secrets, right?"

"We did," he said. "There were things I kept out of sight, or tried to." Taylor's anger, the silence between them, all day it had been like a dull ache in his chest. She was talking and he didn't want that to stop. "She went through hell with me, I guess. The kind of man I am." Taylor looked away from the road, as if trying to see from his expression what he might mean. "The kind that's attracted to other men."

He wasn't sure why he'd said it. To show her how slight her betrayal really was, how much more a marriage could stand. Or maybe it was simple selfishness, a need to unburden himself—a hope that the distance she'd imposed might be narrowed somehow if she knew that this, too, was something they shared. He could tell from her look that she hadn't suspected. Because he was old. Her idea of him, it probably didn't include the sorts of desires that quickened and troubled the lives of younger people.

"So, then, when you and Alma were together," she asked carefully, "did you have other lovers? Did she?"

"Not her. It was my problem. When I met Alma, I thought I was cured. I wouldn't have gotten married if I'd known it would happen again."

"Cured?"

"Sounds peculiar, I know. But back then, that's how I thought about it. It wasn't who I wanted to be, so I tried to stop. But then I'd be tempted. I'd give in. I'd ask her forgiveness and make promises. Then I'd put her through it all again. We stayed together, had our children, and I kept that other part of my life, well, I kept it separate. We didn't talk about it anymore."

"But she knew?"

"She knew who I was. When the kids were grown and out of the house, I offered to give her a divorce. But she didn't want it. Neither of us did."

As the light began to fail, they broke off their search and turned back toward the motel. Pulling into the lot, they found a black Lexus parked next to their rig. Erjot met them at the door.

"Mr. Autry—"

Taylor put herself between the two men, said her name, and stuck out her hand.

"It's Guy's name on the contract," she said. "But half the bees that got taken, they belong to me."

"I see. I have some news about that. But, maybe not out here . . . "

Taylor unlocked the door and they went inside.

"We've been asking around," Erjot said, removing his aviators and hooking them onto the collar of his shirt. "Someone calling himself 'Laki' has been reaching out to the other growers, saying he has hives to rent. My father and I, we think this is the man who stole from you."

Hope hit Guy like a blow to the chest. All through their search, the frantic activity of the last forty-eight hours, he'd never really believed they'd get the bees back. It was just something to keep him from shutting down again.

"One of our friends was contacted. He played me a phone message, and I recognized the voice." As he talked, Erjot fingered the diamond stud in his ear. "His real name is Fetu Leota. Years ago, he did some work for our family. But he started causing trouble, and we had to fire him."

"So, you know where he is?" Taylor asked. "Have you told the police?"

Erjot shrugged. "We could do that. The sheriff will want to go to a judge and get a warrant. But all that will take time. Fetu is a coward. As soon as he senses trouble, he'll run away. Maybe he takes your hives with him." His voice was calm and remote, as if he had more important things on his mind. "His family will hide him. Here or in Samoa. Also, my father, he's old-fashioned. This sort of dispute, he doesn't like to involve the police."

"Dispute?" Taylor said. "We were robbed. Those colonies are worth thousands of dollars. Tens of thousands."

"So," Guy said. "It sounds like you have a different idea."

"Yes." Erjot placed a business card facedown on the table, a number jotted on the back. "Tell him you're growers, willing to pay a high price for the hives."

"Set up a meeting."

"Exactly. Fetu and the hives will be at the same place at the same time. If you find that he's stolen from you, you can handle things however you want." The corner of Erjot's eye twitched, stirring his fine black lashes. He set his sunglasses back on his nose and rose from the table. "What this man did, it was a terrible thing. My father and I, we regret that it happened on our land. But the almonds won't wait to bloom. We can give you two more days. After that, if you don't have the bees, we'll have to get them from someone else."

They met the man calling himself Laki in a suburban neighborhood at the edge of town: a network of cul-de-sacs lined with beige houses, aboveground pools set up in the yards. His fenced-in compound was little more than a split-wing with an attached garage, sitting on an acre and a half of sand and scrub-grass. As they approached the house, Guy saw the uneven rows of palettes, hives stacked two or three high. Most beekeepers painted their boxes white or gray, but these were bright orange, the color of traffic cones.

In the driveway, a middle-aged man in cargo shorts and a sweat-stained polo waved them over. He greeted them with a smile, slapped their backs as if they were neighbors arriving for a barbecue.

"Sorry," he said, "but the AC isn't working right now. We'll be better off out here." He led them to the backyard, a court of sun-scorched grass and a few evergreen bushes clinging to life. There was a trampoline, the sagging safety net half-detached from the poles. Nearby, a miniature plastic chair, the kind used in preschools, lay overturned in the dirt.

They sat at a lawn table. Fetu reached into a cooler and handed them cans of Coors Light. "We can't go higher than two-ten per box," Taylor said, once they'd gotten down to business. Fetu tried to hide it, but Guy could see he was pleased.

"Make it two-twenty and you've got a deal."

"That works for us." Taylor looked at him, and Guy paused, keeping up the act, then reached out to shake Fetu's hand.

Fetu raised his beer. "To new friends, and a profitable partnership." They tapped their cans together. It was all Guy could do not to seize the hive tool hidden in his jacket and see how many of the man's teeth he could pry out.

"Let's make it official," Guy said, setting his beer on the table. "I'll get the paperwork out of the car." A glance at Taylor and he was sure he could leave her there.

He went back around to the front of the house. In the driveway, he bent down and tucked his trousers into his socks; a few stings were inevitable, but he could do without bees getting inside his clothes. Leaving the car where it was, he headed in the direction of the orange boxes.

When he reached the first one, he dropped into a crouch and took out his hive tool. Angling the sharp end above one of the handholds, he scraped off the top layer of paint. Sticky orange shavings clung to his blade, and he reached out to feel the exposed wood. Someone had been at it with a sander, but his fingers could still trace the faint outlines of a four-digit number, and after that, his brand mark, just where he knew to find it.

A popping sound, like the bursting of a plastic bag, echoed through the yard. It was quickly followed by a second pop. It was only after the third shot that he registered the sounds as gunfire. Bees clinging to his hands and clothes, he turned and ran toward the house.

When he reached the backyard, he found Taylor on the patio, both hands gripping a pistol. She had tears in her eyes, from anger or fear, he couldn't tell. Fetu was facedown on the ground, half inside the house and half out of it. The sliding door was partly open, the glass punctured and spidered where two bullets had passed through it. Fetu was down, but Taylor kept the gun trained on him. The smell of gunpowder hung in the air.

"Fuck, I don't know. He must have figured something was up. We were talking and then he flipped over the table, tried to get past me. Go through me. I mean, what was I supposed to . . . fuck, this is bad," she said. "This is so bad . . . "

"It's all right." Guy approached her slowly. "How would you feel about giving me that gun?"

Taylor glanced down first at Fetu, then at the gun. Guy reached out and, slow and gentle, the way he moved when he was working his bees, he placed his hands over hers. Gradually, she loosened her grip, let him wrest it away.

Fetu moaned. At least he was alive. Not that Guy cared whether he lived or died. His only concern was for Taylor. The plan, if they found the hives, had been to call the police. That wasn't going to work now. They'd have to deal with the situation themselves.

"She shot me," Fetu whimpered. "She fucking shot me."

"Is there anybody else here?" Guy said, looking into the house. "Is anybody coming?"

"I'm hurt. I'm bleeding."

"I asked you a question." Guy pulled back the slider and let it go— the unmistakable click-clack of a round being chambered. He took aim at the back of Fetu's head, his thumb finding the safety, flipping it on.

"Up on your knees." Reaching for the doorframe, Fetu complied. Blood seeped from his waist, running down his leg and staining his shorts. Not spurting, though. That was good. Guy had heard three shots, two of which had gone into the door. So, shot once in the hip with a twenty-two, a round better suited to killing squirrels than people.

They'd caught a break, it seemed. This man wasn't going to die; he was barely injured.

"It's my house. It's just me. Please, don't—"

"You got a car in that garage?"

"Yes, yes."

"You're going to get in it. Now."

"Guy," Taylor said, hesitant.

"You're going to drive far away from here," he continued, "and forget this ever happened. We know who you are and we know what you did. The police will too if you don't get out of here right now."

Guy found himself sitting on the couch in an unfamiliar house, a ceiling fan slowly churning the air. His hands were dappled with stings, and he seemed to be holding a pistol. The sound of machinery and shouting reached him and he got up to look out the window. Men dressed for farm work, people he didn't know, were loading hives onto pallets. Another man drove a forklift, transferring the hives to a flatbed truck.

They weren't the right color, but somehow he knew these boxes were his, full of his bees. He was angry, already very angry, though he wasn't sure what the feeling was attached to. Whatever was happening out there, he was going to put a stop to it. Was that why he had the gun? He flipped off the safety.

Outside, the sun was blinding. When he could see clearly, he pointed the pistol into the air and pulled the trigger. It was so light in his hands, made such a pathetic little crack, that he fired a second time to be sure he hadn't imagined it. The men stopped what they were doing and stared. One dropped to the ground, and another dove behind a stack of boxes.

"What's going on here?" Guy demanded. "What do you think you're doing on my property?" It looked nothing like his property. But his hives were here. None of it made any sense.

"What the fuck, Guy," someone shouted. "Put the gun down!"

Shading his eyes, he searched for the source. With the sun at her back, he couldn't be sure, but it seemed to be Taylor, maybe twenty yards away. She was walking toward him, her hands raised. This was wrong, all wrong. He lowered the gun and backed into the house.

As he sat on the couch, certain facts surfaced. He was not in Iowa, but California. His hives had been stolen by a man named Fetu, and this was Fetu's house. The people outside worked for the Singhs; he had been the one to call them. There was a gentle knock on the frame, and then Taylor came to sit beside him.

"Guy, are you okay?"

"I'm sorry," he said. "I was confused."

Without thinking, he wiped his nose on the sleeve of his suit jacket. It had begun to run.

Years later, Taylor drove her own rig, bringing her bees to the Singh's orchard, then moving on to pollinate plums, cherries, apples—even cotton and lima beans. By the time Guy retired, she was doing well enough to buy him out. After that, he kept only the house and a few hives, working them just for the pleasure of it. In the afternoons, he sat in a chair in the yard, the nurse inside if he needed her, and watched his bees.

His feet bare, he gripped the soft grass with his toes. All these years and his love for the bees—his admiration for their industry, the fierceness with which they defended what was theirs—it had not diminished. They served one another and harmed nothing. Was there any human being who could say the same?

One of the colonies was bearding, a thick curtain of bees hanging from the bottom of the hive. Scouts were already on the wing, looking for a new home. Left to themselves they would choose wild and broken-down places over the handsome boxes he built for them. A hollow tree perhaps, or the eaves of an abandoned barn.

In the past, he would have split the colony, placed the new queen and her retinue in an empty box. But there was no need for that now. He'd let them go. A summer breeze brought the scent of pine. The sound of wings, a gentle hum, fading as he closed his eyes.

Two Valleys

SCOTT TOOK MARINO'S place in the pilot's seat, their flight suits hissing softly as they passed. The control stations at Creech were cramped, but Scott knew pilots at other bases, some of them officers, who had to work out of trailers or repurposed shipping containers. He wondered if he'd ever get used to it: suiting up, going over the mission briefing, and then entering a windowless room instead of a cockpit. "So," he said, checking instruments and controls, "any action down there?"

"Only if you count a military-age male leaving his compound at 0200," Marino said, "and then creeping out into the fields."

"What, we think he had a weapons cache out there?"

The sensor operator, a kid named Walsh, snickered into his coffee. His face pallid from the glow of the monitors, he looked like a smirking ghost.

"Naw," Marino said, "guy was taking a shit." He shuffled into the hall and, still chuckling at his joke, closed the door behind him.

Scott brought his focus back to the screens and nudged the flight-stick to one side. Two seconds later and a hemisphere away, the Predator obeyed, tracing a broad ellipse over the Khost Valley. It was the dead of night in Afghanistan, but here in the Mojave, the sun was bearing down on flats of bursage and creosote. The Predator, hangared in Kandahar, had been in the sky for hours. A ground crew handled takeoff and landing, but Scott (or one of the other pilots) took over once the plane was in the air. He hated it when politicians or people on the news called them drones. These were remote-piloted aircraft, and they didn't fly themselves.

Walsh leaned over, one hand cupped to the side of his mouth as if he were about to share some confidence. "Captain," he said, "I think you should know, that tangy aroma of ass you're smelling, that ain't me. That's one hundred percent Airman Marino." As Walsh pulled away, his eyes tracked across the bank of screens. Apparently finding nothing of interest there, he returned to the comic book in his lap. Air from one of the vents fluttered the corners of the pages, but it didn't help with the stink. Bodies sat in these chairs around the clock, men and women both, sweating and smoking and eating and farting for up to twelve hours at a time before they were relieved, replaced by a fresh pilot and a new sensor operator.

As for Walsh, Scott didn't think much of him. Nineteen, maybe twenty, Walsh was just another kid from the Nellis puppy mill. He'd logged his forty hours of basic flight in a Cessna and then spent a few months in a shed in the desert spotting targets and launching warheads full of concrete at broken-down tanks. Walsh may have been certified to fly, but he was no pilot.

At forty, Scott was practically an old-timer at Creech and, unlike some others, he'd served in war zones. He'd flown C-130 cargo planes in Iraq, delivering supplies to frontline troops. In places where there were no airstrips, he'd landed the hulking things right on the highways.

Later, stationed at a base in Bagram, he'd evacuated wounded soldiers from the ground.

But he'd talked it over with Laura, and they'd decided: accepting the post at Creech was the best thing. He figured he was still making a difference. But now, when he left the battlefield, he could be home an hour later, emptying the dishwasher or helping his girls with their schoolwork.

And there were other reasons. His marriage had held up to the five- and six-month deployments overseas and the temporary assignments that took him away from Laura even when they lived in the same house. But this last deployment, a full year in Afghanistan—that had nearly put an end to it.

He'd found himself tuning her out during their video chats, barely able to connect with whatever she was saying about playdates, her weight-loss plan, or her online degree. He'd started resenting the demands for five or ten more minutes of talk when, really, all he wanted was to get some sleep. Near the end, he would keep another window open on the desktop and watch a DVD with the sound turned off. By then, Laura had stopped trying, too. They could be online at the same time, both their cameras live, and not say more than a few words to each other for ten or fifteen minutes.

When he came back, he was quieter than before and less willing to feel things he didn't have to. Laura had changed, too. She'd gotten used to handling the finances, taking care of the kids, taking care of herself. It wasn't clear where Scott fit in anymore. They'd both seen the post to Nevada as a chance to start again, maybe their last.

It was hours staring at the screens. The village was asleep, and the only motion was from a pair of goats that ambled through the alleys between household compounds. At dawn, groups of men began to gather at the mosque to offer morning prayers. Two boys shoveled fuel into the mouth of a clay oven, and a man with a bucket splashed handfuls of water onto the ground, settling the dust of the main road.

Scott received word that the convoy was on its way. He guided the Predator along an updraft, then pointed the nose, with its cluster of cameras, down at the valley. A line of armored trucks moved like a ragged stitch through the patchwork of gardens and spring wheat. The vehicles stopped in front of the iron gate that marked the village entrance, and the soldiers took positions.

There was a rasp of leather as Walsh leaned forward in his chair. "Squirters," he said, "Three of 'em." On the other side of the village, Scott could make out three figures fleeing down a footpath. The sensor switched to infrared and instantly the heat from the men's bodies gleamed white against the black of the landscape. He radioed with the commander on the ground and relayed their position: thirty meters from the rear gate, lying prone in a ditch.

For the rest of the morning, the soldiers went from house to house. Scott and Walsh scanned the hills for Taliban or Haqqani fighters while the riflemen of Icarus company, first platoon, gathered every man or boy who could shoulder a rifle and stood them in a line by the roadside. They patted the men down, checking their long tunics for weapons, then led them to the mosque in the center of town. There they scanned each one, fingertips and iris.

Walsh clasped both hands behind his head, yawned louder than he needed to, and stretched. "Biometrics," he said. "Bad guys can run, but they can't hide." Scott had the urge to seize the kid in a full nelson and pin him, wriggling, to the floor. Instead, he reached over to Walsh's side of the dash and took a mini-doughnut out of the open package. He bit into it, then spat the crumbs and a rind of stale frosting into his palm.

"Jesus, Walsh, how can you eat those things?" He wrapped the mess in a napkin and tossed it in the trash.

By the time the soldiers had collected all the data, he had barely an hour left in his shift. He put his hands to his eyes and tried to rub the heaviness out of them. Just a little while longer, he caught himself thinking, and he'd be on the couch with a cold beer and a game controller. Embarrassed at his selfishness, he turned away from the thought and worked to put all of his attention back on the soldiers, men who wanted to be at home—deserved to be—more than he did.

The soldiers clamored back into their trucks, and he flew the Predator ahead of the convoy. He peered down at what passed for a road: a twisting trail of rutted earth broken by stones and smothered in a fine dust like spent gunpowder. For grid after grid, there was nothing but the buzz of the air-conditioning and the dull sepia of sand.

"Can you come around on that?" Walsh said, straightening in his chair.

"On what?"

Walsh fed him the coordinates, and he coaxed the airframe into position. The craft descended in a gentle spiral, an eye-stippled spider dropping from the hub of its web. Its cameras fixed on the ground, a spot where the road pinched through a dry, high-walled gulch. But the screens only showed a pixelated patch of mud, cracked by the sun and half-buried in silt.

"Okay," Walsh said after a long time, toggling between day TV and infrared. "It's nothing."

Before he knew why, Scott's heart was slamming against his ribs. The first truck had passed through the ravine, but the second wasn't on his display anymore. In its place was a plume of sand and gray-white smoke. The monitors snapped to IR, and Scott could see the flames, white-hot, consuming the vehicle and the men inside.

His headset crackled with the voices of radio operators and the shouts of the other men. "God damn! IED, truck two—Back of my head, it's fucking hurting—It's on. Go. Can you hear?"

"Speck Three-Two copies all," he said. "We'll find them."

He pulled back on the stick and counted—one one-thousand, two one-thousand—through the excruciating delay. The Predator began to climb, showing not just the convoy, but the surrounding mountains and farms.

The shooting will start now.

"I think they're behind that ridge. Motherfuckers—He's hurt bad—I need somebody with eyes on!"

"Roger, Icarus. Working on it."

The front of the second truck had been sheared off and the engine block was yards away, smoldering in the brush. The first truck raced ahead, out of the killzone, but the others were jammed up behind.

Help them, Lord.

The steppes were still and empty. There were no technicals on the road, no mortar teams in the scrub of the cliff tops, no men with rifles and RPGs scrambling out of ditches.

The village.

An old woman swept dust from the threshold of a mud house. In a wooden stall, a shopkeeper butchered a goat. *The fields, maybe they're in the fields.* A figure was crouching, concealed in a patch of green.

"There," he said.

But no. It was just a farmer stooped over stalks of wheat, studying their flowering heads. Text flashed across the chat room monitor: KING COBRA IS MARY IN FIVE MIKES. Marine helicopters were spinning up in Rocket City. They'd be inbound in minutes, but Scott couldn't find anything for them to shoot at.

"Where are they, Speck?" a voice said over the radio. "Where the hell are they?"

"No enemy contacts, Icarus."

He'd watched these men set up a net in the desert and play volleyball, had guided them through the snarled streets of Kabul. Once, when a Humvee broke down on a patrol, he'd kept watch over them as they made camp, maintained a vigil through the night so they could sleep. They'd been grateful for that; they'd thanked him.

But there was nothing he could do for them now, nothing but watch. Fire reached the magazine for the truck's fifty cal and started cooking off the ammo. A shower of pale sparks filled one corner of the monitor. "Hang in there," he said. "Cobra is inbound." It was just past 2300 hours in Nevada when the choppers landed. Then someone tapped him on the shoulder, and his shift was over.

• • •

He filled up at the Shell station across from the base. Its highway sign was busted, the plastic casing torn away and the bare fluorescents shining white. It was grimy and disordered inside, with empty patches on the shelves and boxes of stock heaped in one corner. Waiting for the cashier to ring him up for the gas and a twelve-pack, Scott eyed the Powerball display. Laura liked to play, and some nights they made an event of it, eating popcorn on the couch and letting the girls stay up an extra hour to watch the drawing. But tonight it seemed wrong somehow, and reckless, to invite fortune into their lives like that.

He returned to his truck and pulled out onto 94 South. There were no cars on the road, and past the station and the roadside casino, it was twenty miles of speechless desert before the first billboard. He rolled down his window, and the sharp scent of piñon pine blew in from the Spring Mountains. His high beams took in the scrub of the roadside but climbed only partway up the utility poles. Their tops indistinct, the rank of bare spars resembled a stand of birches stripped and blackened by a culling fire. The foothills were hunched silhouettes at his right, while, further off, the towers of High Desert Prison hung in the air like smoke.

Las Vegas flickered at his left and then unfurled itself: a sweep of golden points, pixel-prickly in the arid dark. Above the hotels and casinos, the beacons of helicopters fluttered like blowing embers. The Luxor, a mountain of black glass, remained tucked away beneath the horizon. Still, he could make out the beam from the pyramid's enormous spotlight, a shaft of silver-white stabbing up at the sky.

He wouldn't tell Laura about the bomb or the men who'd been killed. So much of what he did was classified, and there were regulations, even about spouses. But it was more than that. He'd learned early on, they all had, to take whatever happened at the base, in that other desert, and stuff it in a footlocker. A forty-minute drive gave you time to secure things, to lock them down tight so they didn't bleed into your other life.

He'd taken a class in college, an introduction to logic. The professor had said this thing about noncontradiction: how A couldn't be B and not-B at the same time. But Scott knew that wasn't true—you could be here and over there, deployed and safe from harm. Maybe he was remembering it wrong, or maybe the world just didn't make that kind of sense anymore. Distracted, he missed the turn for the beltway and home.

He took the exit for downtown instead and pulled into the garage at the Golden Gate. He took out his phone and called Laura. She didn't pick up right away, and her voice was coarse from waking.

"I'm sorry," he said, "but I have to stick around here a bit longer."

"What, why? Is everything all right?"

"Sure. Yeah. It's just paperwork, this new intelligence officer. He says he needs this report tonight, that it can't wait until tomorrow, which is complete—"

"It's okay," she said, her voice flat. There was a silence, and he wondered if she might have fallen back to sleep.

"Laura?"

"I saw another one of those spiders in the kitchen tonight, the brown ones. Actually Clara saw it. Rachel screamed and shut herself in her room. I was going to smash it, but it hid under the refrigerator." She yawned. "Did you remember to call Terminix?"

"Shit. No, it slipped my mind."

"Don't worry about it." She sounded resigned, as if she hadn't expected him to remember. "I'll take care of it."

"No, really. I'll call them first thing tomorrow." There was another silence and he listened for the sound of her breathing. There were still times—when she came home flush and glowing from a run, or when she laughed playing some silly game with Clara—flashes that pierced through the dullness and allowed him to feel something like grace, as if, despite his not deserving it, God had entrusted him with something precious. It wasn't too late to talk to her, if he was willing to try. Maybe he'd decided—and stuff the regulations—to tell her what had happened.

"Okay," she said. "I'm turning in. Don't let them keep you too late."

"I love you," he said.

"Love you, too."

• • •

For blocks, the corridor of Fremont Street was canopied by a vault of LED screens, the triumphal arch of some gaudy empire. The monitors displayed a kaleidoscope of designs swirling against a psychedelic background: pulsing yin-yangs and pinwheeling flowers, peace symbols and clip-art lips. The whole corridor vibrated with the force of the speakers. It was a song he knew but couldn't remember the name of: a rich man sidling up to a girl, bragging about his money. Scott's gaze passed over the souvenir shops and casinos, then lingered on a neon sign: a reclining cowgirl kicking up white-booted heels.

Once the bouncer had patted him down, the hostess led him to a long oval counter that doubled as a catwalk. He ordered two Jack and Cokes and stared at the runway, which was padded with red felt and fitted with a colonnade of steel poles. The DJ announced the next dancer and the first licks of "You Shook Me All Night Long" growled out of the speakers. As soon as the drums kicked in, a woman in a G-string strutted onstage and whipped her hair in time with the beat.

What right did he have to be in this desert and not that one. To sit on this stool, or in that box on base, bulletproof in his leather pilot's seat? He finished the second drink and tried to put it out of his mind. Annoyed and unwilling to wait for the server to come around again, he went to the bar himself. What he did in that room, he knew it wasn't valorous. But let some F-16 pilot call him a "cubicle jockey" or a "PlayStation warrior"—and Scott would shut his goddamn face for him. He'd killed, the same as them, except he didn't drop a bomb from forty thousand feet and then rocket off into the sunset. When he launched a missile, he saw it hit. In the harsh monochrome of IR, he watched as the body parts flew into the air. He knew what it meant to wait for the heat to drain from a broken body, to watch a man, a person, writhe in the dirt and then darken until he was the same gray-black as the ground. He knew what it meant to be the cause of it.

"Hey, fella," someone said, "what's with the blank stare?" The voice belonged to a pretty Asian girl. She wore a thin blazer, the sleeves rolled to the elbows, and her breasts, the size of clementines, were banded by the wide straps of a suspender skirt. She held his gaze and took a slow sip from a straw that stuck out from her can of Red Bull.

"A bad day at work is all."

"Want to buy me a drink and tell me about it?" she said. And then, when he hesitated, "It's just a drink."

"Yeah," he said. "Sure." He followed her to one of the leather couches. The corner was dark, lit only by the red glow of Chinese lanterns. The booth's scalloped back hung over them like a carapace.

"I'm Frankie."

"Scott." Frankie seemed to struggle with her blazer, an invitation for him to help her out of it, and they made awkward small talk until the waitress arrived with their drinks.

"So," he asked, "where are you from?"

"San Jose," she said, smiling.

"I mean, you know, originally?"

"San Jose." She crinkled her nose, but the smile didn't leave her face. "My parents, though, they immigrated from Thailand during the revolution. It wasn't safe there."

"Huh," he said. He could find Thailand on a map, but all he knew of the country were the stories a navy buddy had told him about "happy endings" and "Ping-Pong shows" in Bangkok. He decided to change the subject. "You don't seem like the other girls in here. I bet you're putting yourself through school or something like that, right?"

"Aw, you're sweet. I'm almost done with my bachelor's. American history. Also international studies."

He let out a long whistle. "A double-major, huh? Impressive." She laughed again.

"Yeah, well, I'm not as smart as some of the others, but I work hard. Besides, there's a lot of overlap. With American history, you know, so much of it happens somewhere else."

"Rachel, my oldest, she loves history. Me, though, I'm more of a math and science type."

"Oh, you have a daughter? Do you have pictures?"

For a while they talked about his girls and Frankie's younger brother, who was learning to program video games at a technical college. He started to relax. It felt good to talk to a beautiful woman and know it was safe. He could say whatever he wanted and she wouldn't reject him. She was also a stripper, not a woman in a nightclub or a hotel bar. There was no chance things would go too far, that he would cheat.

"I don't usually meet guys like you," she said, taking his arm and leaning against him. "And Scott, I wish I could stay, but unless you want to buy a dance, I have to go. Textbooks aren't cheap, you know?"

He knew the things strippers said to make a customer feel special. If he'd asked her about making rent instead of taking classes, she would have given him the hard luck story. But really, none of that mattered. He was just where he wanted to be. He knew too much to be suckered, but not so much that it ruined the fantasy.

He took forty dollars out of his wallet. "What if I paid you for a dance and we just talked a little more?"

"I'd like that." She kissed him on the cheek, then took the bills and slipped them into her tiny purse. "Hey. I don't even know what you do for a living. Wait! Let me guess—you're an engineer."

He shook his head. "Close. I'm a foreman, like at a construction site. That's actually why I came here tonight, because of something that happened at work today." She seemed so interested, so open, and she'd been so nice to him. He felt he could talk to her. "Two guys on the site. Well, there was an accident. I was supposed to keep them safe, but I couldn't." He stared down at the table.

Frankie put her hand on his thigh. "I'm sure it wasn't your fault," she said. "You're a good man. I can tell." He put his hand over hers, and for a minute or so they sat there like that, not saying anything. He took a deep breath and let it out.

"Thanks," he said, taking his hand away to rub the back of his neck. "Like I was saying, just a really bad day." They talked for a while longer, about her classes and his hobbies. When their time was up, she gave him a hug and kissed him on the cheek.

"Hey, Scott," she said, drawing away and looking him in the eyes,

"I want to tell you something. What I said before. My family's not really from Thailand. They came here from Vietnam." She shrugged. "It's just some guys, you know, they have some bad associations, so when they ask, I say Thailand. It's easier."

He said good night and walked back out into the strobing noise of Fremont Street. In the truck, he checked his face in the rearview, wetted his finger, and wiped it clean of any hint of lipstick. What she'd told him, was it because she'd felt something for him—not desire, maybe, but something she hadn't wanted to mar with a lie? More likely, it was a lure, a souvenir of self-disclosure with the promise of more on some other night. Sincere or not, it had stirred him.

His house was dark, and Laura had drawn the blinds across the windows that faced the street. The house was all right, definitely a step up from the family quarters at Hill AFB, and nicer even than their place in Fairbanks had been. But the yard was an eyesore, a grassless plane of gray-brown gravel. At first they'd talked about adding some flowering cacti and a hedge of sage bushes. He'd wanted to do the work himself, but Laura had insisted on a landscape company. They'd fought about it for a week and then just dropped it and left things the way they were.

Not wanting to set off the garage's security lights, he pulled alongside the curb and cut the engine. There was a low rumble like a distant explosion—the red-eye to Hawaii, most likely—and then it was quiet. He took the twelve-pack from the passenger seat, skulked along the side of the house, and slipped in through the back door. Intent on a shower to get rid of the club smells and maybe a swig of mouthwash to mask the whiskey, he started down the hall.

He'd taken only a few steps when Laura padded out of the darkened bedroom. It was like the dreams he had sometimes of being an intruder in his own home. Except those dreams were in infrared, the bodies of his sleeping daughters transformed into fluorescent bundles that spun white light through the translucent walls.

At the doorway to the bathroom, Laura stopped and looked over her shoulder. He caught his breath and stood completely still. He couldn't stand for her to see him now, a feckless soldier who'd failed to protect his brothers. A man who no longer went to his wife for counsel or comfort but instead paid some strange girl to tell him lies. For a moment, she squinted into the dark. Then, either seeing nothing or choosing not to see, she turned and went into the bathroom.

He kept his eyes on the door and, feeling along the wall, took a few steps back before rounding the corner and stepping into the kitchen. He waited several minutes after the toilet flushed, then switched on the light. He took the beers from the counter where he'd left them and made room in the fridge.

A tawny blur twitched at the edge of his vision. The thing scuttled a few inches across the counter, then stiffened. Laura had left a wine glass in the sink, a few purplish dregs still stuck to the bottom. He seized it by the stem and brought it down, trapping the creature in a clear, vaulted cage.

The spider, with its woolly fangs and convulsing limbs, disgusted him. But he willed himself to lean close and peer down into the glass. The spider's abdomen was the size of a nickel, sandy brown, and covered with fine, short hairs. A dark mark, like a brand in the shape of a fiddle, covered its head and back. Not a daddy longlegs, then, or a garden spider, but a recluse.

The thing was revolting, but he wasn't sure he wanted to kill it. It didn't belong here, of course, and he couldn't allow it to stay. Still, he thought about slipping a sheet of paper under the glass and putting the thing outside. He wanted, maybe just this once, to be merciful.

But if it got back in somehow, if it bit Laura or one of the girls. . . . He couldn't take the chance. He searched through the drawers until he found the long-necked lighter, the one he used for the grill. He tipped the glass and slid the tip of the lighter beneath it. The recluse ran to the nozzle and began to climb over it, probing the vents with its slender legs. When he pulled the trigger, the creature jerked away from the spout of flame with such force it tore off one of its own limbs. It curled the others against its body and lay still, a whitish mess blown out of its side.

The severed limb jerked senselessly around the scorched spot on the countertop. Something caught in his throat watching it. He pulled the trigger again, holding it until there was nothing more to see.

All at Sea

for Abi

LIE AND SAY YOU have to pee. In his bathroom, check your purse for the condoms and then list, in alphabetical order, every kind of lie you can think of: barefaced lie, big lie, bullshit, fabrication, fib, lying through your teeth. At "half-truth," relax the rules and make the list into a little tune set to "Ebony and Ivory": mendacity and perjury / self-deception, half-truth, and perfidy. Of course you're forgetting the worst one—no, not really forgetting. More of an omission.

You're about to tell him. You have to tell him. It's probably required by law or something. People are always making crazy laws. If you don't say anything and he finds out, would it be a civil matter, or could they send you to prison? Prison... all that time to draw. Flush the toilet and fantasize about your new life as an inmate, how your story goes viral and launches your career as an outsider artist.

Don't forget to run the water.

In the living room, kneel at the foot of the couch and slip your hands under his shirt. His chest is firm and hairless. Wonder if he shaves it. Roll one of his nipples between your thumb and forefinger and savor his hoarse sigh. When his shirt is off and you're on top of him, just as he is fumbling with the clasp of your bra, that's when you brush your lips against his neck and murmur, "Wait."

Beneath the skinny jeans and hipster posturing, this man is tender, inexperienced, and at least five years too young for you. He has probably spent more time considering the qualities of craft beers than puzzling over the meaning of consent, but he has older sisters, and he is not a bad person. He stops when you ask him to.

Say: "Before we go any further." Tell him, "There's something I need to . . . " Anxiety, a prickly flower, blossoms in your chest. Say: "I'm positive."

His mouth opens and closes like a fish gulping air. His fauxhawk is a khaki fin, bobbing gently on the tide. Wish you hadn't waited this long to say something, that you didn't like him so much already.

Take his hand. Trace the letters into his palm like it's a secret message, a love note passed in health class: H-I-V.

Reach for his belt buckle. As you press your hand against the front of his jeans, ask: "What do you want?" It's like a fairy tale. You're cursed, and you can't break the spell yourself. Someone else has to say the right words.

Ask him again.

It's what they all say, reciting from *The Nice Guy Handbook*, Chapter Thirteen, "How to Reject a Girl with the Plague": "I guess I'm just not feeling it anymore," "I have to get up pretty early tomorrow," "I think I'm still hung up on my ex." What they don't do is give you a chance to explain what "undetectable viral load" means or how you've managed to live with this for so long.

Did you really think it would turn out differently this time? You keep forgetting: You're not the princess in this story. You're the poison apple.

Find your bag, delete his number from your phone, and take the Blue Line to the aquarium. It's free on Thursdays and doesn't close for a couple more hours. On the train, remember the way your grandmother used to squeeze your hand. Three times, once for each word: *I—Love—You.* Wonder if you'll ever be loved like that again.

The shark tank is closed for renovations, and the artificial reef, with its hand-painted polyps, just reminds you of all those colonies bleached to bone by a warming ocean. Even Shelby the sea turtle lacks her usual buoyancy. She lurks at the bottom of her tank, a scuttled igloo, working over a scrap of cabbage with her fleshy beak.

Claim a bench in front of the coastal habitat case and begin to sketch the fairy penguins. A colony of pygmies, the birds are tiny, blue, and iridescent. Their feathers shimmer indigo as they preen in the floodlights, dimming to slate when they shuffle into their shady burrows (one for each mating pair, the label says). One of the birds thrusts out its chest, struts in a circle, and brays. Think this must be Franco, the one from the subway ads, his photo captioned "The Ladies Man."

But then again, maybe not.

Despite the aquarium's citywide "Penguins with Personality" campaign, you have to confess, they all look pretty much the same to you. The same short gray beaks and foam-white bellies, the same pink-cake-frosting feet. Close your sketchbook and consider the possibility that this is a symptom of a much larger defect, an inability to see the world in its particular and manifold splendor—and isn't that what an artist is in the end, a person who can see?

And if you're not an artist, then you're just a "good drawer" and no different from those hacks at state fairs who make sketches of people with tiny bodies and enormous heads—people on Rollerblades or skateboards, their attention divided between swinging tennis rackets and reading the Bible. Consider that you may be the same as your mother and your sisters and everyone else, with no special power to transform your private humiliations, the stupid suffering of your life, into something better.

For Christ's sake, will you stop crying?

"Excuse me," someone says. Then, "Maggie, is that you?"

Turn to find a spindly boy in a denim shirt staring down at you. There is a blankness to his look, like someone who has just been in an accident. But there's more to it than that. It's a receptive, good-hearted sort of blankness, a vacancy that suggests openness, a capacity to abide among uncertainties. He has a lopsided grin and his hair is scruffy and blond. Decide that he is not un-cute.

"It's Zach," he says, sparing you having to ask. "From, you know, the place."

God, Zach. You haven't thought of him in months. Two years ago, Zach had been a mistake, a nuthouse romance you'd gotten yourself into during a seven-day stretch at McLean for generalized anxiety disorder.

"Gad," the intake counselor had said, reading aloud from your file. Funny, you'd thought, how that little verb could encompass so much of your life. Wasn't that just what you'd been doing? Gadding about, rambling idly from park to library to movie theater, your mind locked in a state of intransitive dread that refused to attach itself, directly or otherwise, to a single object?

And then, tonight at the aquarium, you compound the mistake. Freshly forsaken and near-psychotic with loneliness, you snivel and cry and spill your guts. Zach sits with you on the bench and agrees with everything—*yes, people do treat each other like wolves; and sure, that dating site, the one for people with HIV, it might be worth a try; and of course, if things get really bad (well worse, anyway), you could always pick up stakes and move to Oregon or, in extremis, do that thing you've been fantasizing about: leave everything behind, your apartment and all your possessions, and go off to live in a shipping container.*

Zach is so affirming, such a surprising source of comfort. When he leans in and puts his arm around your shoulder, you do not move away.

At home, change into sweatpants and order takeout. The radio is tuned to the college station, and the kid at the controls is playing a single album without commentary or interruption. It's Nirvana, you think, the one with the medical model on the cover, the indecency of her organs held in place by clear plastic.

Remember when those songs were new, when Marcus made you that first mix tape. Remember Marcus. *Marcus Calidus, Marcus Crispus Dorsuo.* Hot-headed boy, he of the curly hair and broad back. You used to steal glimpses of him in the lot across from the school, where he stood with his friends, impudently smoking. Shifting his weight from one leg to the other, his elbow flexing as he brought the cigarette to his lips, he'd had the cool perfection of a Greek statue come to life. He finally noticed your looking, and within the month you were riding in his car, helping with his homework, and teaching him the Latin names for every part of him you loved: *musculus deltoidei, rectum abdominus, frenulum preputii penis.*

There were other girls: girls who took his hand at bonfires and allowed themselves to be led into the woods, and the ones he bedded on trips to see his cousin in the city. At least that's what you imagined. For a long time, you didn't really want to know. But then you did, and it was easy, insultingly easy, to catch him.

In his car, you shouted and cried, then ordered him to pull over and let you out. You went the rest of the way on foot, five or six miles along the shoulder of Route Seven and then a shortcut through the pastures to your house. You went straight to your room and didn't tell your sisters or your parents a thing about it. Instead, you pretended to be sick the last two weeks of school and, when summer came, only made trips into town to buy CDs from Second Spin and take out books from the library.

The rest of the story is almost too painful to remember. Marcus going away to join the army and then coming back to live in his parents' garage. The sound of his voice as he told you, between choking, childlike sobs, about the physical exam and why the army wouldn't take him, the desperation in his voice as he begged you not to tell anyone. Then your test, the cheap molded plastic of the waiting room chairs, the ringing in your ears so loud when the nurse gave you the results that you weren't sure if she was speaking or just mouthing the words.

If you have to think about it at all, it's best to think about the sex. How the two of you, convinced no one would ever want you again, fucked until you were sore. And then fought or cried, and then fucked some more. You're starting to salvage a fantasy out of the wreckage of those memories, considering whether to go into the bedroom to get your vibrator, when the buzzer sounds—an ear-splitting, gut-clenching clang that sends you dashing for the door-release button.

Take a look through the peephole and find something familiar about the face, some essence untouched by the fish-eye effect of the lens—the way it flares the nostrils, stretches the ears to the antipodes.

"Maggie," he says when you open the door, "don't be mad, okay?"

So, not the delivery guy, but Zach, who, stepping inside, fills your apartment with the olfactory bouquet of a fresh-from-shift's-end aquarium custodian: the ammoniac tang of seabird guano anchored to a foundation of brine-ripened lichen, and, fluttering between these, heart notes of Murphy's Oil Soap, that not-unpleasant savor of freshly polished horse tack.

"I guess I should have called first," he says, "but I wanted to see you. And look, I brought you something." He unzips his coveralls and produces a lady's evening bag, a knock-off Fendi sort of number, its surface bristling with blue fur.

It is clearly a bag for a crazy person.

Is that how he sees you? Crazy Maggie? Maggie, the crazy bag lady? But then he turns the thing over and you see it's not a bag, but a stuffed animal: a bird with a white belly and puffy pink feet.

"It was like fate or something," he says, standing the plush creature upright on the coffee table, "seeing you again."

He'd been thinking of that night the two of you sneaked out of the redbrick dorms (yours filled with neurotics, his a melting pot of border-lines, skin-pickers, and the acutely impulsive). Together, you'd stolen away to the shelter of an oak grove on the hospital grounds where you'd talked for hours and made out like teenagers. On the walk back, you'd worked together to wrench a plastic owl from its perch on a garden shed and, smuggling it into the group room, placed the decoy on a high mantel shelf. The next morning, during the mixed therapy session, you'd stifled giggles and shared secret looks, waiting for someone to notice.

And then tonight, alone in the aquarium, he'd been spraying out a chum bucket, emptying the contents into a grate in some nonpublic area, when the realization struck him like the bump and bite of a shark attack. He could feel it now, what must have been there all along, this cosmic connection between the two of you, a gene-deep imperative like the one that drives those little birds to make their nests together and pair up for life.

He'd dropped hose and bucket then, and instead of locking up the gift shop, absconded with a stuffed penguin from the window display. Taking a leap of faith that you actually lived at the address you'd given him on your last day at the hospital—the one to which he'd sent letters and postcards and handcrafted mail art, all without reply—he'd fired up his Honda Civic and driven across town to your door.

Tell him he needs to slow down; he's talking so fast. Notice your own breath quickening and think how strange it is, this susceptibility you have to other people's moods. Know that whatever happens, you must not give yourself over to his unhinged energy.

Show signs of improvement. Tell him thank you for the stuffed animal and for listening at the aquarium—that helped a lot—but you're hungry now, and tired, and, to be honest, his showing up like this in the middle of the night is kind of scary. He's scaring you.

Ask if he remembers all that talk at McLean about setting appropriate boundaries.

Say: "You can't just show up at my house. I mean it."

Boundary set.

Think you may have said the words out loud: "Boundary set." Wonder if that's how it's supposed to work, like casting a spell or raising shields on *Star Trek*. Or is it like when a judge says "guilty" or "not guilty," and in that irrevocable instant, reality is transformed? But then you're not a judge or a starship captain, and words alone won't protect you.

Zach looks hurt and bewildered, but he's going. On the front stoop, he asks if he can call you tomorrow, or in a couple of days?

Say "maybe" and shut the door. Set all the locks and watch from behind the blinds as the twin beams of his headlights sweep across your window and into the street.

After he has gone, and the Chow N' Joy delivery guy has gone, and the world outside has been shut away behind the deadbolt and the door guard, you're finally free to unfold the take-out containers' white cardboard petals and consume your promised double portion of Hon Sue Gai with rooster sauce.

Brush your teeth and get ready for bed. Take one five-milligram tablet of Olanzapine, two forty-milligram capsules of Fluoxetine, and of course the Atripla, its film-coated surface dyspeptic pink and stamped with the numerals 1-2-3. The clean-smelling immunologist had called it a "drug cocktail," a phrase that promised way more fun than swallowing a full gram horse pill every night.

Think of that Greek word for medicine, *pharmakon*, with its double sense of "tonic" and "poison." Or are you mixing it up with *pharmakoi*, one or the other a term for those deformed people kept like pets in Hellenic city-states. Well, at least until a plague or some other crisis came along, at which point the townsfolk would march the *pharmakoi* (*pharmakeus?* well, whichever) to the edge of the city, and then beat their genitals with fig branches until the poor, cast-out things expired. Turn out the bathroom light, resolving to go online in the morning and sort out the mix-up.

Sleep through most of Friday and then, in the afternoon, finish falsifying the week's unemployment forms. In the Work Search Activity Log, indicate that you have, as mandated by the Massachusetts Department of Labor, engaged in multiple work search activities, on multiple separate days, using no less than three different job search methods: Monday, answered a Craigslist posting for a job as a taxidermist's model. Wednesday, attended "Running with the Big Dogs" long haul truckers networking event at Natick Service Plaza Eastbound. Thursday, offered up holy hecatombs to the never-dying gods and prayed aloud for a position as an adhesives company sales representative.

The penguin (Roxy, it says on her tag) still sits on your coffee table, accusing you with her shiny, black-button eyes. Unlock your phone and find the Wikipedia entry for fairy penguins. The page is full of useful information, some of which must be true. The birds are nocturnal, it says, and have a wide range of calls. Though not endangered exactly, they have a surfeit of natural enemies: sharks, seals, gulls, weasels, feral cats, oil spills, bottle packaging. Imagine the game of *Clue, Fairy Penguin Edition*: Roxy the penguin, strangled in the bathtub by the weasel with the ring from a Coors twelve-pack.

List your natural enemies: insomnia, self-doubt, phone calls from your mother, your immune system, boys with cruel eyes. Click through to the marine conservation chart and decide that you are a G3: globally vulnerable and at high risk of extinction in the wild. Feel strangely comforted—you are no longer alone, but part of a tribe, your fate linked to that of the Mississippi pigtoe, the old prairie crayfish, the frecklebelly madtom.

Realize you've been stalling, putting off leaving the apartment to meet Zach across town. Wonder why you agreed to the date in the first place. Though, on reflection, it's not hard to understand. It's nice to be wanted, even by the unbalanced, and whatever his issues might be, he already knows about your status and the trouble you have just being in the world, and he's never been weird about it. He's been great, in fact. Besides, you tell yourself, it's one drink, a casual meeting in a public place. Nothing to get worked up about.

Unless, of course, this ardor for you turns out to be more than free-floating libido looking for a place to land, more than the passing mania of a boy who isn't taking his meds. It's unsettling to imagine there is something inside you that you don't know about and can't see, some *thing* that has set off these feelings inside him.

Arrive late and find him already seated at the bar. Take a moment to enjoy being unobserved, the one who gets to look. He is wearing a car coat from the seventies, saddle-brown leather with too-short sleeves that ride up to reveal wrists ringed with freckles. Jeans cling to his runner's calves, tapering to bony ankles and frayed canvas sneakers. He is talking to a pretty twentysomething, a girl with green hair, tattoos, and surgical steel punched through her earlobes, each fleshless tunnel defining a void the size of a newborn's fist. Become aware of an immediate hatred for her.

Direct your attention to the mirror behind the shelf of liquor bottles. Your face is still youthful—or, at least, not yet old—your skin tanned to a pale fawn from days given over to aimless strolls around the city. Your eyes, though, they seem duller and deeper-set than you remember, the skin below them blue-blotched and creased. One of your lids, the left one, seems to be drooping. A pretty face given all that, but expressionless, a late-night cashier at a grocery store. Wonder when it was exactly that you started looking so hapless, so tired.

Zach glances over his shoulder, then vaults off his stool. He calls your name and hugs you for much longer than is proper. It's awkward at first, being held by a boy you hardly know. His arms are stronger than you remember, and after three seconds the first tingle of panic shimmers down your spine. It's like one of those UFC matches Marcus used to watch, the kind that end on the ground in a tangle of limbs, one of the fighters writhing in the grip of some colorfully named submission hold—the Inappropriate Anaconda, the Uneasy Ascot, the Flying Double First Date. A moment later, the feeling changes again, to something like relief, the taut cords of muscles warming and untwining. But then it's all just too much, and you have to break away.

He has a fresh bruise on his cheek, below his left eye. Remember two years ago, braced against an oak tree, touching that face in the light of a quarter moon. Experience a fresh surge of tenderness.

"It's nothing," he says, "I caught an elbow at a hardcore show."

Be certain he is lying.

Follow him to the dark-stained bench and squeeze in behind a table.

As the waitress takes your order, trace your fingers over the pair of initials scored into the wood, the rough-hewn heart enclosing them.

Take sips from your stout and catch him up on the last two years. Your health has been good, and it looks like it might stay that way, at least for as long as you can keep paying for the drugs. The anxiety, too, has been under control, despite a week last summer when it was too frightening to leave the house, take a shower, or answer your phone. You lost your job at the deli after that, and then your favorite cousin— the one you told him about at McLean—well, he went alone into the woods one morning and shot himself. Mostly, though, you've been doing much better. You've started drawing again—sketching, really, but then he already knew that.

Take this opportunity to affirm that, despite evidence to the contrary, you are not prone to public weeping these days, nothing like before. He takes everything in, seemingly without judgment, his eyes never leaving your face. It's both validating and off-putting, this unremitting attention.

He doesn't ask any questions, but instead, apropos of nothing, informs you that the jukebox is broken, that it's been stuck on free play for weeks. Is there anything you want to hear? Leave the table and stand, hip to hip, in front of the old machine. Press its fat beige buttons and flip through the racks of postpunk standards. With his arm around your waist, lean forward and punch in your selections: "Pictures of You," "How Soon Is Now?," "Love Will Tear Us Apart," the maudlin anthems of your youth.

Have another beer, then switch to bourbon. Crack up at one of Zach's stories, something about dropping acid and a fountain in Las Vegas. When the lights come down, notice that the barroom, a single corridor, has filled up with people.

Lean your head on his shoulder and stare into the mirror above the bar. It is the wall of an aquarium, its shadow-smudged surface a portal into a place filled with unfathomable creatures. Watch them as they glide through a world in which you cannot breathe.

Finish your whiskey and instigate a pointless, one-sided argument. Say: "So, Roxy, what was that supposed to mean, anyway?"

"Who?"

"Roxy, the penguin with personality."

Inform him that you're nothing like that, and never will be—some flightless bird he can spring from its cage, a mate-for-life he can carry off to some grimy one-bedroom burrow.

He's making that face again. The wounded incomprehension of the wrongly accused. Guess that he is the kind of man ultimately incapable of seeing himself as anything but innocent, the sort of person who believes that, in the end, good intentions are all that really matter. Or maybe that's just how his face looks.

Kiss him before he says something stupid.

It's not as good as the first time, lacks the thrill of stealing away from your captors to meet in secret, the tartness of transgression. You can also discern an unpleasant eagerness in the movements of his tongue, its anguished probing. Why does he need so badly for you to feel him? Is it to prove that he exists? He should know by now that people can't do that for each other. At least not for long.

Outside, conceal yourself in a shadowed spot in the bar's back lot and share the joint Zach produces from his jacket. It takes only two puffs to discover that this weed—a variety of locally sourced, hybridized, and hydroponic kush—is a different vegetal entirely from the parched schwag of your dorm-room days. Try to wave off the offer of a third hit and find that there's been some kind of breach between volition and action, as if signals from your brain must now traverse a great gulf before reaching your limbs. When your arm does begin to move, the gesture has a flip-book quality, a consecutive layering of discrete frames, each overtaking the one before it, contributing its variation to the global illusion of motion and time.

Become aware of a mouth moving over your neck, your ear, a tongue finding its way to your lips, pressing them open. Do your best to kiss the mouth back, though it feels like a muscular worm in your mouth.

Cold hands press up against your hips, move up to the wire of your bra. In a spasm of modesty, look over Zach's shoulder into the lot, scanning for any movement among the parked cars.

When he drops to his knees and moves his mouth against your bare belly, a mix of kisses and murmurs—"love you," "so hot," "make you feel good"—determine that things are moving much too fast. Kissing is one thing, but the weed is making you nauseous, and under no circumstances are you having sex with this boy in a parking lot.

Shake your head from side to side. Say "Mm-mm," the closest thing to "no" you're capable of articulating with this much THC in your system. Grope in the dark for his face. As he undoes the top button of your jeans, get hold of his chin and draw him up.

Off his knees, he rises into a crouch and lifts your shirt. Kissing his way up your front, he slips his hands up and under your bra. You're able to make a wider variety of noises now—the groan of a sleeper who doesn't want to wake, the whimper of a kicked dog, the snarl of a wolf caught in a trap. But words still won't come, and your muffled protests have no effect. How is it that he can't or won't understand?

His hands and mouth, they're so relentless; it's like fending off a predator. Wish you were an octopus, capable of releasing a cloud of ink. With a jet of water, you'd launch yourself away from danger, tentacles trailing behind you, your three hearts pumping hard in the boneless chamber of your chest. Or maybe a starfish, able to shed its limbs. If only you could detach your right arm and flee, leave it behind as a horrifying distraction. Remember reading somewhere that the abandoned arm can go on growing, eventually transforming into a new creature altogether. How cruel it would be, and sad, giving up this other you, this limb daughter, to fend for herself.

A car door slams, and then another. A few feet away, an engine is turning over. Headlights strike the side of the building, the beam's reflection illuminating your hiding place like a flash of lightning. Zach takes your hand and leads you onto the sidewalk.

Walk together for a few blocks without saying anything. When he asks if you're okay, yank your hand away and run into the street. Find, miraculously, that your legs are working again, well enough at least that you can stumble between the cars waiting at the signal light and traverse the stairs leading down to the subway station. You can hear him calling your name from the platform, his voice echoing through the station as you step through the closing doors of a Red Line train.

Wish tonight that you could be anything but human. How was it you were born to this, to be caught up in all this needless complexity, to be both possessor and object of so many desperate desires? How much better it would be to live at the bottom of the ocean.

Make up your mind that, in fact, the thing you'd like most to be is an anglerfish, a she-devil of the sea. She lacks the defenses of *Octopoda* and *Asteroidea*, but then again, she doesn't need them. She is not prey, but a carnivore, cruising the ocean floor and unhinging her jaw to swallow creatures twice her size. Her mouth, a cavern crowded with bands of inward-pointing fangs, prevents any escape from the smooth-walled cell of her stomach.

Evolution's darling, she doesn't waste time looking for a mate. The males of the species are stunted, parasitic, and so minuscule that she carries whole colonies fused to her flanks and fins. She is led on always by her body's own light, a blazing phosphorescence, both lantern and lure, beaming a path through the deepwater dark.

Decide you could live in the world like that, you really could.

Fault Trace

CARTER WAS halfway back to town before the landscape, miles of bare trees and high-tension wires, yielded something of interest—a low cliff cleaved in half by a roadcut. He dropped his speed to well below the limit, allowed himself time to admire the outcroppings of orange-brown stone, the oldest exposed rocks in the region. Wind and water had long ago stripped away the softer, clay-rich strata, leaving behind shelves of limestone, their layers resembling sheets of baked filo.

He tried to see the place as it had been in the Carboniferous. Driven to the equator by continental collisions, the plateau had been warm and humid year-round. What was now snow-clad hill country had once been an alluvial plain, its deltas and wetland forests subject to the cyclic surges of an inland sea. The brackish lake that formed these outcrops had been home to burrowing mollusks, flea-like crustaceans, gilled proto-snails, and scallops that propelled themselves through the water with claps of their fan-shaped shells.

Conceiving a world hundreds of millions of years past, straining to project his consciousness across that inhuman interval—it inspired in him a near-religious awe, threatened to put him in a kind of trance. His surroundings began to blur and recede, the present moment redshifting as it hurtled away. A silver SUV grew large in his rearview and swung out into the passing lane. The driver leaned on the horn, the sound Doppler-distorted as he charged ahead.

Carter had gotten used to the idea that other people couldn't or wouldn't see the land the way he did. During their first trip to Woodbridge, he'd pulled off at just this spot, insisted that Sharon and Kenzie get out of the car and take a closer look at the rocks.

"This isn't the kind of limestone you'd find on a seafloor," he'd told them, "left behind by shell-builders." He'd stood on his toes, reached out, and ran his hand along one of the crevices. "This is micrite, built up by chemical precipitation in the water column."

Kenzie lingered a few steps behind him, arms folded tightly across her chest. Her earbuds were in and she was wearing that nonexpression he'd come to call her "zombie face": mouth turned down, eyes heavy-lidded, a blank gaze that flickered now and then with unconcealed contempt for her stupid family. Sharon waited near the car, bored and benevolent, her face shadowed by the brim of a large sun hat.

He'd wanted to tell them everything he knew about that other time, to conjure for them that place that was still this place, transposed over the present. An alien world, but as real as the rough stone against his fingertips. But Kenzie no longer cared what her father had to say about a pile of rocks by the roadside. And Sharon, forbearing Sharon, she'd known who she was marrying. If she no longer found his enthusiasms endearing, she was at least still willing to indulge them.

It wasn't fair to expect them to share his passion for the planet's history. He understood that. But the distance was still painful. In that moment he'd felt, as he had only a few times before, how alone he was

within his family. He hadn't said any more, just withdrew his hand from
the rock and walked back to the car.

He came to a rolling stop at the signal light, rumbled over the redbrick
crosswalk, and parked at the meter in front of his office. Setting down
the grocery bag, he lifted the security shutter—installed last week after
someone pitched a brick through the display window—and let himself
in. Throwing out a carton of spoiled milk, he made room for Kenzie's
things in the refrigerator.

He'd been halfway to the office that morning when he'd remembered the grocery list. Most of the items could be had at Kroger, but
his daughter's commitment to food ethics required the purchase of
esoteric products that most of the good, stout people of Woodbridge
had never heard of. For these, he'd had to drive to the Phoenix Moon
co-op, two towns over and forty minutes out of his way. He hadn't
expected to see anyone he knew there. But then he'd caught a woodsy,
citrus smell, heard a young woman's voice.

"Mr. Geddes? I didn't know you shopped here." It was Cindy Jensen,
Kenzie's English teacher. She'd caught him off-balance, lost among the
cartons of unsweetened flax milk, the packages of chickenless nuggets,
searching for the things that would please his daughter.

"Wow," she'd said. "Kenzie. She's so passionate, so driven—and
smart, *so* smart."

"You know, she's not eating any meat or dairy these days," he'd said.
"Of course her mom and I remember when she used to eat hotdogs
right out of the package."

Cindy had kept on, as if speaking only to herself. "She has this fire.
I love that about her. At the same time, though . . . " A look of concern
passed over her face. "I wonder, has she talked to you at all about 'Up
for Debate'?"

The question made him cringe. Embarrassment, mostly, but beneath
that, there was sadness, too. The truth was that Kenzie didn't talk to
him about much of anything anymore.

The conversation had upset him, and he tried to put it out of his mind. Shutting the refrigerator door, he felt a tug, like the force of gravity, from the bottle of Scotch nestled in his desk. He couldn't say exactly when it had become impossible to face the day without his morning cup of whiskey. Not long after the town hall meetings, he supposed, the editorials in the *Woodbridge Tribune* decrying what oil and gas development was doing to the region. The Wayne National Forest stood a few miles east of town, and anyone with a grievance against Umbra Energy, some objection to the lawful use it was making of forest land, they laid it on Carter's doorstep. He couldn't pick up a prescription or fill up at a gas station without fielding complaints about truck traffic and clear-cutting.

He could sympathize—at least to a point. Just like them, he had to deal with the occasional tanker truck hogging a narrow thruway or a flatbed loaded with machinery bearing down on a one-lane bridge. During peak production, eighteen-wheelers thundered down the roads, their oversize loads pounding asphalt back to gravel. The grousing by people who hiked and fished in the Wayne, that too was understandable. There wasn't much point trying to commune with nature within a five-mile radius of a drill pad. Birdcalls, the sounds of a free-running stream—these didn't stand a chance against the revving of diesel engines and the constant hum of compressors.

His real problem was with the environmentalists. They'd gotten the locals riled up about water contamination, convinced them that drilling was going to shake loose trapped methane, free it to bubble up and foul the aquifer. That footage of people in Dimock setting fire to their tap water, that was all most people knew about hydraulic fracturing. When people asked him about Dimock—which they always did—he told them the truth. It might have been caused by fracking, but even if it was, problems like that were the result of carelessness: cheap materials and shoddy work by outfits looking to cut costs.

Umbra, on the other hand, had done everything by the book. He had made sure of it. He'd insisted on the best casings to line the well bores, overseen the cementing himself. At first, his bosses had balked at the expense. He'd gotten into shouting matches with the CFO. He'd threatened to quit. But in the end, his budgets were approved; he ran the sites his way. The residents of Woodbridge were arguing with the wrong person. He'd been as much of an advocate for clean water as those Sierra Club people. Really, they ought to be thanking him.

He went to the sink to wash out his coffee mug. The words PAPA BEAR were still legible across the cup's face, but the silhouette of the loping grizzly had faded. A Father's Day gift from Kenzie, it was a relic of another age, a time before she'd turned resentful and strange. Retrieving the bottle from its hiding place, he poured himself a double dram. He coaxed some water from the tap, just a splash, allowing it to draw out the bite of apple, the barley sweetness. Mug in hand, he looked out his new front window. It was still early, and things were quiet. His building, a converted storefront, shared the block with antique shops, a flag and pole store, and the office of a state rep known for his straight-A report cards from the NRA.

Across the street, the armory blocked his view of the river trail, but he knew Sharon had passed that way on her morning jog. He imagined her running, breath in rhythm with her steps, her lungs releasing gray-white blossoms of carbon dioxide. Before leaving the house, he'd taken a moment to watch her through the kitchen window. She'd been out on the deck in her tights, stretching her legs against the railing, the left one strapped into a brace. She ran in spite of the tingling and burning in her feet, the occasional falls. He worried, of course, but he also admired her for it. She'd never been willing to give up on anything, even him.

He'd have to talk to her about it tonight, the conversation with Cindy Jensen. Apparently his daughter's class had been debating abortion, and whatever Kenzie had said had upset her classmates, especially the YWAM kids, the ones who prayed at the flagpole each morning. This, in itself, didn't concern him. In fact, he was proud. Kenzie's tendency to overthink everything was mostly a source of alienation and annoyance to him. But using her intellectual gifts to stir up a room full of self-righteous teens—that was something he could get behind.

But now, it seemed, the administration was concerned, afraid of an outcry from the prayerful parents of the Ebenezer Seventh-day Adventist Church. Those Ebenezer people. They had grown men and women believing that the earth was made in six literal days, convinced that the entire geological and fossil record had been falsified, that scientists were part of a diabolic conspiracy meant to lead them astray. Completely irrational. As far as Carter was concerned, people like that should have to wear signs. A scarlet *I* or something. At least that way, you could see them coming, know what you were dealing with before the conversation started. He'd told Cindy all this, but she'd only smiled nervously and backed away, pulling her cart along with her.

Was it possible that she hadn't agreed? She was a teacher, wasn't she? She'd been to college.

"Well, I don't know," she'd said. "I just wanted to mention, about Kenzie . . . "

Bewildered, he'd watched as she spun her cart around and pushed it briskly in the direction of the express checkout lane. The people in this part of the state, they were so different from the city dwellers in the north. He couldn't blame Kenzie for hating Woodbridge, resenting him for bringing her here.

But then, what else could he have done? He would have been happy staying in Columbus, keeping on with Good River Development, working for the Boyd family as the company's VP. But the market for gas had tanked, and Umbra Energy had offered a way out. The Boyds had agreed to sell, and the new owners had given Carter a choice: move to Woodbridge and become lead petroleum engineer for the Utica play or collect a modest severance and try to start over. It wouldn't be long before Kenzie headed off to college, and Sharon's condition was getting worse by the year. They didn't talk about it, but there would probably come a time when his wife would have to give up her career and go on disability.

He'd taken the deal—of course he had. Though it had meant uprooting his family, taking charge of fracking operations for a company he didn't believe in, people he didn't trust. Kenzie would understand when she was older. In real life, purity was seldom an option.

He turned away from the street and retreated to his office. A windowless back room, it was a third the size of his old one. To get to his desk, he had to maneuver past the boxes of files that lined the walls, a chair stacked with books and reports, and the occasional rock sample, stored in a repurposed yogurt tub. He opened his battered laptop and started in on the morning report, an account of the last twenty-four hours of drilling: well depth, rig time, supplies used.

The receptionist wasn't due in until after noon, so there was no harm pouring himself a second Scotch. He'd just stepped out from behind his desk, taken his first step forward, when something shoved him so hard that he stumbled. On his bookshelf, a binder tipped and fell with a vinyl smack, then another, then the whole row. A few more steps and he got hold of the doorframe. In the window display, the ornaments on the office Christmas tree—glinting blue and red bulbs—swayed gently from side to side.

The whole thing lasted maybe five seconds.

He stepped out onto the sidewalk where Darlene Bump, owner of the flag store, stood digging in the pockets of her star-spangled jacket.

"You, too?" she said. "Thought maybe I'd lost it." She produced a vape stick and started puffing. "What do you figure, a little earthquake?"

"Not likely." His mind went immediately to the grimmest possibilities. A train derailment, its tank cars filled with crude oil. A pipeline explosion, the gas-fed eruption shooting flame eight stories high. Or, worst of all, an accident at one of his wells, the kind that could burn men alive.

It was cold, and only a few people had stepped outside to investigate. On the corner, a pair of men in puffy coats tapped excitedly on their phones. A woman in front of the antique shop stood with her head bowed, her gloved hands folded in prayer. Across the street, something let out a muffled, animal sound. Leonard Granger was lying on his side on the frozen turf. Carter downed the last of the Scotch in one gulp, set his cup on the windowsill, and ran across the street.

"Bastards," Leonard said when Carter and Darlene reached him. "Arrogant bastards." They tried to help him up, each taking an arm, but he cried out in pain. "It's my shoulder, goddammit," he said, wriggling into a sitting position. "Clean out of the socket."

Carter lowered into a squat and gripped the old man around the middle. "Come on, Leonard. On three." He pushed upward, but with too much force—he hadn't expected the man to be so light in his arms.

On their feet, they had momentum to spare. Winter slush, damp grass—his smooth-soled shoes couldn't find purchase. Darlene, her sturdy body moving with sudden grace, clasped them both in a bearhug and held them upright.

When she let go, she was grinning. Carter had seen her fake smile before, many times—the customer-service smile, the midwestern-nice smile—but not this one. He steadied himself on a parking meter, breathing hard but smiling, too.

"It's the fracking," Leonard said, scowling. "It's Youngstown all over again."

"Oh come off it, Leonard," Darlene said. "We don't know what happened yet."

"You think I can't tell an earthquake when it knocks me to the ground?" Leonard winced, cradling his arm. "You're a witness, Darlene." He jerked his head in Carter's direction. "I'm going to sue the pants off these bastards."

Leonard had been a critic of Umbra from the beginning. At one of the town halls he'd dressed up in a Batman outfit: vinyl cape, utility belt, the nosepiece of his mask painted white. "Umbra Energy," he'd chanted. "Bad for bats! Bad for trees! Bad for you and me!"

Though Carter had appreciated Leonard's sense of spectacle, he hadn't paid much attention to whatever it was the man had been ranting about. It had been Kenzie who'd told him about white-nose syndrome. Bats in the region were under threat from a fungal infection, a snowy fuzz that grew on their piglike snouts, disturbing their hibernation. The result was confused, skinny bats, whole colonies driven too early from their caves. They roosted in the trees of the Wayne National Forest, foraging for insects and burning through what was left of their winter fat.

A population crash was coming. If Umbra kept cutting down trees to make way for pads and pipelines, the bats would have to range even farther to find shelter. Most wouldn't make it. Kenzie hadn't been nasty about it, but her accusation—implied rather than stated outright—had been clear: "The bats are dying, and it's your fault."

"Want me to call you an ambulance?" Carter offered.

"I'll drive myself," Leonard said, stalking off.

Carter scanned the horizon, sniffed the air. There was no trace of smoke. He thought of texting Sharon. But then he imagined her at the library, fielding calls from residents who wanted to know why the ground was shaking. As for Kenzie, she was at the high school, and they'd never been those kinds of parents, ones who texted their kids every time there was a tornado watch.

He followed Darlene as she recrossed the street. Maybe it was the Scotch, or because she'd taken his side against Leonard, but he felt a new camaraderie with her.

"Think he'll be okay?" he asked.

She took a draw from her stick, then blew a cloud of grape-scented steam. "That man shouldn't be driving anywhere, not on a suspended license." Darlene was married to the sheriff and knew everyone's business. "Dustin pulled him over last week, up by Sugar Creek," she said, shaking her head. "He was tripping balls."

The drill site was loud and dirty. Trucks came and went, gears grinding, stirring the eight acres of gravel that served as the floor of the drill pad. The wind was up, and Carter was glad for his safety glasses as he passed through a cloud of blowing snow mixed with silica sand. Roughnecks on the rig shouted over thundering engines. The stink of diesel fuel was everywhere.

Dominic, the tool pusher, was leaning against his office trailer. He had a piece of wood in his hand and was carving at it with a folding knife. Though he stood a foot shorter than Carter and was technically a subordinate, Dominic was a Texan and an ex-marine, and Carter had always found him intimidating. Mostly, though, he had a friendly admiration for the man, his directness and good humor. When he reached the trailer, Dominic put away the knife. They shook hands and went inside.

"I guess we had some excitement this morning," Dominic said, setting the chunk of wood on his desk, a half-formed figure of a horned owl. When he took off his hard hat and glasses, Carter could see his cheek was bruised. One eye swollen.

"Is that how you got that headlight?"

"Oh, this? Nah." Dominic filled two Styrofoam cups with coffee and handed one to Carter. "Here's a story for you. A new guy on the day tour, real quiet. He'd been coming in all week wearing this hat. It was bright pink. The other guys were giving him shit—saying he must be a sissy or a queer. Somebody said they'd seen him crying and that made everything worse. I guess he'd had enough. Took a swing at the motor operator. All hell broke loose and I had to get in the middle of it." Dominic finished emptying sugar packets into his cup and took a sip. "Turns out the guy has a wife back in Harrisburg. Breast cancer. His sister-in-law, she has it, too."

"That's awful. Anybody getting fired over it?"

"Nah. Nobody's dead or laid up, and it's no worse than what they get up to on their off-hours."

The coffee was stale and bitter. Carter leaned forward and set it on the desk. "So, the seismic event. Any trouble on-site? Before or after?"

"A little ground shake like that?" Dominic gestured to the radio behind him. It was tuned to a classic rock station, the music muffling the racket outside. "I heard somebody on the call-in show complaining about a picture falling off the wall. But out here, we have trucks that rumble worse. I doubt anybody even noticed."

"And—it's stupid, I know, but people are going to ask—were we drilling at the time?"

"Good news for you there. A bit had worn down and we'd just finished the tripping. We had the string back together and down the hole, but we hadn't fired it up yet."

The hole was a vertical shaft a mile-and-a-half deep, straddled by the drilling rig, its mast a four-story tower of steel. Once they'd hit the brittle black shale of the Utica play, Dominic and his men had started digging sideways. Every five hundred feet, they stopped drilling, laid the pipe, and fracked the stage. When the pumps stopped and the pressure was released, the well spouted a toxic slurry of fracking fluid mixed with brine. It was this sludge that Carter was really worried about. Or more precisely, the deep injection well, a few miles down the road, that was used to dispose of it.

"All right, Dominic," he said. "I've got another stop to make. Appreciate the help."

Dominic walked him to the car. Above, at the top of the rig, an American flag snapped in the wind. Umbra outfitted all of their rigs with flags. A little free goodwill, a reminder that they were an American company, doing their part to reduce the country's dependence on foreign oil. Carter found them gaudy, a cheap appeal to sentiment. He wondered what Dominic, a veteran of the Iraq wars, thought of the flags, but he'd never had the nerve to ask.

"Chin up, man." Dominic clapped him briefly on the shoulder. "We don't know anything yet."

The injection well was much smaller than the drill site, a fenced-in area about the size of a football field. Behind a low wall, nine cylindrical storage tanks stood in upright rows. A brine truck was parked nearby, the driver outside the cab, his attention fixed on a hose that drew his fluid cargo into the tanks.

Carter had selected the site himself, picked out a formation of Devonian-age sandstone to store what flowed back from Umbra's gas wells. Four hundred million years ago, what was now a forest had been a shallow sea. The sand at its bottom had settled, been compacted by the layers above, and turned to rock. But a porous rock, with many gaps, perfect for soaking up the toxic backwash that gushed from the drill sites.

He wasn't happy about the rate of injection, the pressure required to pump hundreds of thousands of gallons into the formation every month, but Umbra was fracking plays up and down Ohio, Pennsylvania, and West Virginia. The waste had to go somewhere, and his well had capacity to spare. He was in no position to turn those trucks away.

Unless, of course, the pressure had caused an earthquake. Which was possible. If the sandstone had been overstressed, the force of the injection could have reached all the way to the basement rock, struck an unmapped fault line. Despite all the denials by lobbyists and PR firms working for the industry, things like that did happen. A four thousand percent increase in earthquakes in Oklahoma over eight years? There was nothing natural about that. He had to admit, it was possible that Leonard Granger was right, that Umbra Energy—that Carter himself— was to blame for the morning's quake.

Still, best for now to believe it had been a natural event. As sound a hypothesis as any other, given what was known. The geology was complex out here, and surveyors made mistakes. There could be an active fault, one that no one knew about. The fact that there were no records of quakes in the region, that didn't mean there'd never been one. Carter knew better than anyone that geological processes happened over vast timelines. Histories, however, those were set down by humans, a species whose existence encompassed no more than a finger-snap in the life of the planet. And really, how could it be anything but natural when he'd been so careful, done everything by the book? It didn't seem fair.

Besides, a single quake meant nothing. There would have to be three or four, a swarm. And didn't he hate it, the way people tied themselves into knots over what were really empirical questions. Of course, there would always be questions that required speculation: What principles should we use to organize society? What is the right way to live? But for everything else, there was scientific inquiry, observation and measurement. And in a pinch, when the data was missing or ambiguous, there was probability. Facts, not opinion—that was how a rational person dealt with a rational universe. But then, the sweat breaking out on his brow, the racing of his heart: these, too, were facts.

. . .

"You forgot the reusable bag again," Kenzie remarked as he set the groceries on the counter. She'd made herself a nest on the couch with oversize pillows and a rayon-filled comforter she'd bought with her own money. (Since the move, she'd shunned the family's other bedding; it might contain down, she'd informed them, very possibly plucked from the bodies of live ducks and geese.) She'd already changed out of her school clothes and into her domestic uniform: plaid PJ bottoms and one of a rotating series of shapeless sweatshirts. The cat, a tiger-striped stray she'd coaxed from under the porch and enlisted as her familiar, had settled into his usual place on her lap. The cat kneaded the tops of her thighs, his eyes pinched shut, thrumming audibly.

Sharon was at the stove, stirring a simmering pot of curry. "Can you check on the quinoa?" she said, releasing the wooden spoon and shaking out her hand. Her neuropathy had been acting up. Sometimes her hands would burn; more often they'd go dead and she'd have to fumble through the day wearing invisible mittens. When it was really bad, her grip would be too weak to lift her morning coffee or, after an hour of typing, her hands would seize, curling into claws.

He removed the lid from the saucepan. A coconut-scented mist whirled upward and then dispersed, revealing the grains inside, light and fluffy. The transition to vegan-friendly dinners hadn't been nearly as difficult (or as tasteless) as he'd feared. Sharon had found recipes online that took thirty minutes to prepare, and they'd both adjusted. Woodbridge was decidedly deficient when it came to Indian and Thai food (his favorites), so he looked forward to curry night.

He switched off the burner and took Sharon's hand—her skin so rough in the winter months—and gently massaged her palm. Most likely, this did nothing to relieve her symptoms, but it had the virtue of at least acknowledging her pain. She shook a dash of cayenne over the pot and shot him a half smile, a sign that, though she appreciated his efforts at affection, she had other priorities at the moment. Releasing her hand, he kissed the back of her neck and left her to her task.

"Is that diesel?"

"On my shoes, I bet—I had to inspect one of the drill sites." He slipped off his wing tips, sniffed at the soles, and set them in the hallway.

"Did you feel the tremor this morning?" she said when he returned. There was a forced mildness to her tone, but he knew what she was really asking.

"Maybe." He ran the water over a tomato and placed it on the cutting board. "I'd look for another letter to the editor from Leonard, though." He diced the tomato and slid the cuttings into the pot. Having made his contribution, he proceeded to the dining room and swung open the carved wooden doors of the liquor cabinet to claim his reward. He selected a tulip-shaped Glencairn glass, a keepsake from a trip to the Laphroaig distillery, and poured out a dram of smoky, peaty Islay whiskey—much too fragrant to drink at work, beyond the powers of breath mints or mouthwash to mask.

Gingerly, he reached over the first row of bottles. Grasping Sharon's vodka, he slid it to the front of the cabinet. More likely to appeal to a seventeen-year-old palate, it was better bait for a trap. He closed the cabinet doors but didn't lock them. In another house, with another teenager, that cabinet would have to be secured.

But Kenzie Geddes didn't sneak drinks from the liquor cabinet. She didn't stay out past curfew or get unauthorized piercings. In fact, her refusal to rebel unnerved him. He longed for some misstep, some domestic infraction for which he and Sharon could rightly admonish her. He wasn't above manufacturing an opportunity, helping things along. Beneath Kenzie's even-tempered assent to her parents' rules, his daughter actually harbored deep resentments—especially for him. He was convinced of it. But she was smart, even devious, playing the adolescent's version of a long game, finding ways to confound her parents without opposing them directly. It was like living with a sleeper agent. He wished she'd just get it over with, show them the knife.

Sharon called from the kitchen. "Kenzie, set the table, please." Kenzie sighed, and the cat, sensing an imminent disturbance, jumped to the floor and trotted to a favored spot next to the radiator. Sharon came into the dining room and, regarding the glass in Carter's hand, wrinkled her nose. "Maybe go easy tonight?"

A few minutes later and they were seated around the table.

"How was school?" Sharon asked.

Kenzie skewered a cube of carrot and lifted it from her bowl. "Well, there was an earthquake during biology." She placed the carrot, luridly orange, between her teeth. She withdrew the fork and chewed, a haughty expression on her face.

"Was anyone hurt?"

"Some of the church kids started praying, and then Melissa Hewitt was speaking in tongues. Josh Billings fell out of his chair, but he's always doing that. He likes the attention." Dabbing at her mouth with a napkin, Kenzie looked at Carter across the table. "But then Mr. Podemski, he said this really interesting thing. He said there's never been an earthquake in Woodbridge before. That's odd, don't you think?"

The aw-shucks lilt to her voice, the way she inclined her head as if perplexed. He wasn't buying it. Did she really think he'd let her humiliate him at the dinner table, force him into a talk about Umbra and the earthquake before he'd had a chance to marshal his arguments? He could outmaneuver her with expertise if he had to, deploy scientific skepticism as a bulwark against blame. But that would be a last resort. Better to change the subject, to show he had gambits of his own.

"That reminds me," he said, "I saw Ms. Jensen at the co-op. She said there was some trouble in English class this week?"

Her face flushing, Kenzie took a long drink of water. "It wasn't my fault. I was just being honest."

Check, Carter thought. It was the same rush he used to get playing chess with her, cornering her king and compelling her to abandon one of her textbook strategies. Never mind that she usually won anyway. Eventually, they'd stopped playing. As Kenzie improved, it had become embarrassing for them both: how consistently and spectacularly she beat him.

"Pro-life, pro-choice, the terms of that debate, they're so played out. It's all so beside the point, but of course nobody can see that." There was a catch in her voice, as if she might begin to cry. "Instead they call you a 'baby killer' and send you pictures of fetuses."

"Someone is calling you a baby killer?" Sharon asked. "Kenzie, honey, I need you to tell us what this is about."

Kenzie closed her eyes and nodded. Opening them again, she exhaled, her breath leaving her body in three ragged little shudders. Carter felt a sudden twist of pain in his chest. Love and anger—an instinctual urge to rush from the room and out onto the street, to track down the people responsible for his daughter's pain, and beat them with his bare fists. He hadn't been prepared to feel any of that. He got up from the table, headed for the liquor cabinet. He needed his glass not to be empty.

"We voted on team captains for the debates. Marissa nominated me and everyone went along. She told them not to worry about it. 'It's a group grade,' she said. 'Kenzie will make sure we get an A.' The rest of them, they barely helped."

"You did the whole project yourself?" he asked. "Cindy—Ms. Jensen, she let that happen?"

"Not exactly. We spent a couple periods in the library, and they brought me things. Kristen took really good notes. But it was the same old stuff—fetuses aren't people, women have a right to control their bodies, reproductive rights and the constitution. That's all true, but it's just so unoriginal. I know those arguments, and the other side knows them, too. If we're just going through the motions, point counterpoint, why bother to have a debate at all? I mean, if it's just a . . . her-rustic."

"Heuristic," he corrected.

Sharon glanced at him. The briefest of looks, but enough to tell him he wasn't helping. He leaned against the liquor cabinet, feeling miserable.

"So, honey," Sharon said, "what is it that actually happened?"

"I told them what I thought. Abortion should be legal, of course.

That's a given. What I'm saying—what I said—is that it's not enough that women be allowed to have abortions. They should be encouraged to have them. I told them I'm not pro-choice, not really. My position, it's pro-death."

Carter and Sharon exchanged looks.

"Our brains, they're wired for optimism, you know? They trick us into thinking our lives—all human lives, I mean—are way better than they are. But if you look at it from the outside, they're so awful. There's so much suffering, even in the best ones, that being born is always a negative. I might as well tell you now," she said, placing her napkin on the table, "I'm a misanthropic anti-natalist."

A misanthrope. Carter had a series of images to go with the word—a sneering, wild-eyed Johnny Rotten shouting "No future for you!"; dirty-haired men wandering through train yards; a mass shooter coldly changing the magazine of a military-style rifle.

"So, you're saying that you hate everyone," he ventured.

"Not individually. But as a species, you have to admit, we're a total disaster. People are so destructive—to animals, to the planet, to each other—and I don't think we should make any more."

"Kenzie, listen to me." Sharon reached across the table and took her hand. "Do you ever think about hurting yourself?" Carter winced. He wasn't sipping his Scotch anymore, but downing it in little, burning gulps.

"Like, am I suicidal?" Kenzie rolled her eyes. She pulled her hand away, easily breaking Sharon's grip. "I don't want to die. I want to get out of this town. I want to go to college." She sighed, as if having to explain something to an exceptionally simple child. "Just because no lives are worth *starting*, doesn't mean that none are worth living. I'm here—I exist. You already made that choice for me. The damage is done. But bringing a new person into this world, knowing how they're going to suffer—well, I think it's selfish. In fact, I believe it's morally wrong."

So they'd been wrong to bring her into the world? Feeding and clothing her, was that another mark against them in her ledger? The idea was outrageous. What she was saying, it was no different from some other girl crying "I never asked to be born" and slamming her bedroom door. It was a cliché, a juvenile complaint dressed up as a logical proof by Kenzie's overheated brain. If she was in trouble with the school, if her classmates were calling her names, he'd be there to stand up for her, offer a shoulder to cry on. But if she wanted him to submit to some kind of self-flagellation, to feel guilty for bringing her into the world, that wasn't going to happen.

And Sharon, surely she wouldn't stand for this. She had as much right to be offended as he did. He tried to catch her eye, but his wife, her face contorted with worry, was entirely focused on Kenzie.

"And honey, you're thinking about this—and it seems like you've really thought about it a lot, probably more than your father and I have—you're thinking about it now because of something that's happened? Is there something you want to tell us? You can tell us anything, you know—"

"God, Mom. *No*. I'm not pregnant, if that's what you're worried about. The 'something that happened' was that I got born. It's like I'm marooned on this planet where all the people and animals are suffering every second, and everyone just goes on making it worse. Do you even realize how fucked-up the world is going to be when I'm your age?"

"Language," Sharon said reflexively.

"Cities underwater, hurricanes, heatwaves and droughts and wild-fires that last for years, pandemics, climate refugees—a billion people running or fighting just to survive. Who would bring a child into that world?"

"Us," Carter said. "We did. That's what you're getting at, right? And the state of the world, I suppose you're owed an apology for that, too? All our doing."

"Half the carbon in the atmosphere, Dad, it's from the last thirty years. You do the math."

There it was. Finally, out in the open, a chance to defend himself. Fracking was killing bats and polluting the water? His profession was immoral? His industry had fucked the planet, left it teetering on the edge of habitability? Horseshit. He'd heard enough—from Leonard, from Kenzie, from all of them. It was time to put a stop to it.

"*Do the math*," he said, scoffing. "Are you kidding me? I don't know where you're getting your numbers, hon, but they don't add up. Do you want a fire to cook with, a warm house in the winter, streetlights? Well, solar and wind, they're never going to cut it, not the way we live now. We could go nuclear, but I can guess what you'd say to that. So, what's left? We burn gas. Unless you'd rather go back to coal. Sure, why not? Dynamite the hills, dump the rubble into valleys and streams—that's never caused any problems."

"Carter, I don't think she's saying—"

"You should hear yourself—'Do the math.' I'm a goddamned engineer!" he said, nearly shouting. "You know what, if you're such a whiz kid—if you've got all the answers—we've got a whiteboard in the garage. I'll get it—you can solve a Darcy equation for radial flow. Really show me how it's done."

"Stop this, Carter. Right now," Sharon said. "I mean it."

He could see that she did. He was sweaty and angry, the liquor working on him. Kenzie stared straight ahead, tears standing in her eyes.

The cat let out a guttural yowl, the same sound he made before depositing a dead mouse at their feet. Galloping through the dining room and into the kitchen, he dropped low and shimmied under the refrigerator.

A muscular wave passed beneath Carter's feet. He tried to steady himself on the liquor cabinet, but it too was wobbling, the bottles and glassware inside softly clanging. Something large and ceramic struck the kitchen tile, shattering.

And then it was over.

Sharon and Kenzie sat in silence, the same stunned look on their faces. Carter staggered the few steps to the table and dropped ungracefully into his chair. What was the point of his arguments, his pleas, now that the earth itself had borne witness against him? What use was there in winning, knowing that his daughter—however she expressed it, with whatever abstractions or qualifications—regretted being alive?

"It's going to be okay," he said, not sure exactly what he meant: the earthquake, the fight at the dinner table, the trouble at school, the planet? He wanted to say how sorry he was—for all of it. He wanted now to offer a different kind of proof, evidence of his conviction— impossible, but true—that he would stand with her, love her, past the time when heat trapped in the atmosphere withered the jungles, or acidic seas ate away the fragile shells of oysters. Beyond the age when rodents the size of elephants stomped across the savannas, and sentient squids, creatures with no memory of fish, skimmed the reefless seas. Until history itself came to an end, was compressed into strata, rock streaked with veins of black—the remains of human lives, transfigured.

Mythology

FIRST, THERE IS the flood. It rains for three days and drowns the yard. Your shirt off, you're a white-trash Hercules, arms inscribed with sailor's tattoos. A surge takes my tricycle, sweeps it past the patio. You lift it, one-handed, from the flow.

After the fight, Mom takes me out of the room. I swear to her: when I am big enough, I am going to kill you. I find a teacher to show me how to breathe, the right way to make a fist. I break boards with my feet, save up for special jeans endorsed by Chuck Norris. But then, you shave off your moustache, and it's like you're a different person. It doesn't seem fair, punishing this new father for the sins of the old one.

We have dinner with the TV on, pork chops and green beans. The sky above the desert is black with smoke. War could come at any time, Dan Rather says. My civics teacher makes us read the papers, and I heave my facts onto the table. This, I am saying, will not be a good war. You tell me to shut my mouth. Do I think I'm so smart? Smarter than the president and his generals? You're not special, you say, in a voice so loud it carries for twenty years.

After the divorce, I see you on weekends. You lie on the couch, drink beer while I sit, bare legs folded, in front of the Nintendo. I cut my hand on something you've left lying on the floor, the rusted tip of an arrow. We never went hunting, you say, still wishing for a different kind of boy. You move away, remarry, speak with pride about your wife's cousin, a boy who is not your son. Every year, for Christmas and my birthday, you send a card with a picture, a wallet-size portrait of yourself, so I don't forget.

You meet your third wife online, a foreigner. You cross the sea, bring her to your house like the spoils of war. It's fine for a while, but then she stops cooking, doing the cleaning. It's like she wants you to starve. You call in the middle of the night and hold out the phone while she yells in her language. See now, you say, what I have to deal with?

You call to give me the news again. Larry, your friend from the navy, has just died. Every week, the same Larry. You're not going to the funeral. Your wife has claimed the good car and left you with a beat-up Honda Civic. You don't trust it to make the trip. And really, who could blame you, a Lazarus like that, expecting tears and fresh flowers every Tuesday.

Your wife calls. In the city where you live, there is a terrible storm, branches blocking the road and the grinding howl of tornado sirens. You're not going to the basement—hang the weatherman. And your wife, what does she know about midsummer storms? You sit on the back porch with a beer, watch as the wind makes waves over the surface of the pool, raindrops batter the tomatoes in your garden. When I get you on the line, your voice is gentler than usual. You tell me about that time in St. Louis, the flood. You think I don't remember, but I do.

The Death of Elpenor

There was one, Elpenor, the youngest man,
not terribly powerful in fighting nor sound in his thoughts.
—THE ODYSSEY, BOOK X, 552–553

ELPENOR WAS a heavy sleeper, and I had to shake hard to wake him. Slipping an arm under his shoulder, I hoisted him to his feet. Together, we padded past our slumbering shipmates, their bedrolls scattered across the richly tiled floor. At the entryway to the high-columned hall, we strained like beasts in harness against the cool bronze doors until, at last, a tapered shaft of moonlight wedged them open.

Outside, we braced a ladder against the porch's eaves and climbed the sturdy rungs to the roof. Our cloaks spread on the slant of river-polished stones, we took long swallows of the wine we'd clipped from Kirke's stores. The same vintage the goddess poured each night into our borrowed cups tasted finer from the lip of the skin. It was tangy with pine sap and stank of goat, but at least you could taste the hand of man in

74

it. A fine, cool night, even under foreign stars. But then, without my asking, Elpenor started in again about the acorns.

"I'm telling you, you can't imagine the taste, not with a man's tongue."

"What other tongue would I have?" I rolled over, drawing the cloak across my shoulders.

"When you bear down, the skin holds for a moment. But then it splits open, and you take that first snout-puckering bite—I can't describe it."

"Then don't."

Elpenor had been soft-headed to begin with, moody and too fond of wine. A fleet runner with a young man's eyes, he'd at least made a tolerable scout. But a year on Kirke's island had ruined him.

Seduced by her singing, he'd followed the others into her lair. My mates—the guileless asses—they sat at the witch's table and drank from bowls brimmed with poisoned mead. She waited until they were glutted and sleepy, then drew her wand. The dread goddess pricked their backs with sprouting hairs, cramped their fingers into hooves, and cast their varied features in the same swinish mold: wide snouts between their pale, squinting eyes.

Out of the whole party, I'd been the only one with the wits to hold back. Unseen, I sped to fetch their rescue. Odysseus, our captain, he made peace with the goddess and compelled her to undo her curse. The men wept for joy, spread their arms, and embraced. Only Elpenor stood apart.

"But the flavor isn't entirely bitter," he kept on, "there's something gentle, almost sweet, at the end."

"I've eaten acorns before." I sat up and brought my legs close. Seizing the bottom of my tunic, I tugged it over my knees. "You might've known that."

"And the Carya nuts, the shells were like bones boiled through the night in a cauldron—and with such sweet marrow inside."

"I must've spoken of it." The wine was working on me now, and though I'd suffered his nonsense for a year, pity was giving way to something hotter.

"But my favorites? Those were the berries from the dagger tree; it makes my mouth water just to think—"

"Enough! I've heard all this." My cheeks red, I pitched him a spearman's glare. He knew better than to say more.

I adjusted the brooch at my shoulder and gathered my tunic so that it fell in a ripple of orderly folds. Elpenor's jacket was frayed and crusted with his own salt; it hung loose about his middle like an empty sack. Was it any wonder that the rest of the crew shunned him, a filthy and tiresome fool?

"Honestly," I said, "I don't know why you can't be grateful. It's true, Kirke wronged us once, but that's all mended now. What we would have given at Troy to dine each night on meat and honeyed wine—and in the hall of a goddess. If you longed for home like the rest of us, I could understand it."

"It's not that."

"The goddess took pity on you. To leave behind the world of men? To eat swill in a filthy sty, and no words to tell of your suffering? I would rather sink to the bottom of the sea than bear that."

"I didn't suffer. I didn't know. She led us into our pen and gave us—"

"Delicious daggerberries!" I shoved the sloshing skin into his hands. "I don't want to hear any more about it. The way you go on, don't you know it's disgraceful? A swine's pleasures aren't fit for a man."

"They were fit enough for me when I had them."

I tried to remember what he had looked like at the beginning, before our hands were blistered from turning oars and hefting spears, before scars traced crooked paths across our limbs. There were times I still thought of him as that clumsy, copper-haired boy who had cried belowdecks and could not be comforted.

But ten years of war had wrung the boy out of him. His muscles were lean, hard cords, wound over his bones like ropes round a spar's end. Most of his hair had fallen away and what was left, a ring around his sunburnt pate, was twisted and tan with filth.

"It's not disgraceful," he said, plucking at his beard.

"What now?"

"Zeus throws off his scepter and takes the form of a bull. All so he can pin some unlucky virgin under his hooves and ravish her. He's the lord of all the gods. Who are we to call it disgraceful?"

"I was talking about you. Leave the gods out of it."

"The deathless ones, why would they make themselves into beasts if there wasn't something to it, a pleasure or casting off that even they long for? Think of it. Memory, speech, custom, law—to heap them all in some forgotten corner and go out on all fours with no master but your own blood."

Tiring of the argument, I listened instead to the rapping of a tardy picus bird. Unaccountably awake, he kept on gouging his beak into some piece of dead wood. I wondered if the boy really was beyond helping. Whatever queer spirit had taken hold of him that day in Kirke's hall still had him in its grip.

"You know," I said, "we were having a fine time before you started jabbering like a barbaroi. As if any but a barbarian would willingly trade his lot for that of a pig. And what about a pig's end, have you thought of that? One day a rough swineherd binds your feet, hangs you from a tree, and gashes your throat while you squeal and kick."

"You talk like it's better for us." He wore a drunken smirk, but his eyes were mirthless.

I couldn't deny it. We'd seen scores butchered at Troy. Chariots unjointed their limbs and ground their bones to meal. Spears smashed through their temples. Swords unspooled their guts in the dust. I wondered what they would think of us, the ones who had lived, talking this way.

"Besides," he said, "beasts aren't like us. Whatever they know of death, they learn it by dying. There's a freedom in that."

"Freedom? What nonsense! Never mind his death—a swine's life isn't his own. He must stay where he is penned, go where he is goaded, and give his flesh for the table when man—*man*—wishes it. The basest slave has more license."

"Tell that to fleet-footed Achilles." He tilted back the skin and wine slopped from the corners of his mouth. "A man like that, with his end decreed by prophecy? He had no more freedom than a horse driven on by a whip."

"A man and a horse, equally free? A fool knows better." I rose to my feet, but above me, the sky wobbled. "Your mind is wild," I said, "an unpropped vine that's gone too long without the reed's correction. It grows tangled and fruitless thoughts. I don't know why I go on trying to husband you." Sopped in wine, I swayed like a new-fledged oarsman. "Help me find the ladder, will you? The light's failing."

"Are you going?"

The clouds parted and I peered down into the courtyard. I could just make out the form of a drowsing lion, one of Kirke's pets, a wide paw draped across its muzzle. She stirred and, gazing up, fixed me in the light of two green-glimmering beacons. Frightened, I returned to my seat.

"You're not wrong," I offered. "Not completely. Fate doles each man his ration of suffering, it's true, but that's not the end of it. When men rage, when they're lawless, when they speak blasphemies, then the deathless ones add to their miseries. Take Achilles, for a lesson. Or look to Odysseus, still so many leagues from home."

I yawned and blinked at the stars. "But why ruin the night worrying over other men's prophecies? The augurs don't know our names and as long as we don't offend, what cause do the gods have to look in our direction?"

Elpenor smiled grimly. "The princes of the earth use us well enough."

"Agreed. But still, we're men, not horses. When we fulfill our oaths, when we show valor and endure hardships, it brings us honor. But when a charger storms into battle, gnashing an iron rod and driven on by the lash of the whip, it's senseless to talk of honor then."

"Or of shame if he flees."

"Yes, but why worry yourself about that? We were courageous— some more than others, to be sure—but to a man, we fought hard. For years we rowed and marched, and at the end we won for them as many captives and as much gold as they could carry off. They owe us honor and—mark me now—that debt will be paid." Elpenor looked down at his hands. When he raised his head again, his face had fallen in anguish.

"We tore an infant from his mother," he said, "and tossed him from the ramparts. We cut down a faultless girl to appease Achilles's selfish ghost." His voice began to falter. "And for what? Because we were frightened and because they told us to. I've searched, I've tried, but I can't find the honor in it."

Dread curdled into anger and again I sprung to my feet. "I don't cry tears for Hector's heir—and yes, we did what we were told. What should we have done? We've been steadfast companions to our captain, faithful servants to our lords."

"Not always faithful."

"What was that?"

"We," he said, looking up. "*You* . . . not always faithful."

"What would you know about it?"

"I don't want a fight. It's getting late."

"Ungrateful slanderer! Who was it that lifted you out of the muck when you fell? Not faithful. Who looked after your unshielded flank, guarded your life against the death-dealing Trojans?"

He shrugged, indifferent. I seized him by the arm and cuffed the back of his mangy head. "I've wasted years bringing you up and damn you, I'll be answered."

"Let go of me," he said. "You're in your cups tonight."

"Speak! Or by this hand, I'll split you against the bricks. I'll leave you for the wolves—yes, by this hand—not a stone, or a fistful of dirt to cover you." Disgusted, I turned him loose and took up the wineskin. I tilted it back, but there were only dregs.

"When the rest of us were captured," he said, "bound by Kirke's spell, the captain asked your counsel. Do you remember what you said?"

"I don't have to—"

"You told him to sail away." He laughed to himself, as if he still couldn't believe it.

"You've no cause—"

"We've been here a year already and I have two ears like everyone else. Did you think I wouldn't hear? They call you a coward, Eury, a mutineer. You told him to leave us behind."

I cringed to see my deed delivered, bare and unlovely, before me. I wanted to toss it away and disown it, find a mantle of fair words to cover its raw nakedness. But I was stripped of speech and couldn't say more.

"So you don't deny it?"

"Yes, I pleaded with him not to lead us to our deaths. You would have done the same if you had any sense." Blood rushed hot behind my eyes. "And who are they to be my judges? Let them judge him, then, 'brilliant' and 'godlike' Odysseus. How many lives do you think he's destroyed with his rashness?"

"Speak lower," he said, looking over his shoulder.

"I will not. Strip him of his titles and his tricks, and that man is nothing but a wild and lawless scoundrel—and everyone would know it if he didn't have a devious mind and a tongue for treachery."

"He's your captain, and a kinsman besides."

"A kinsman? He's kept me from my wife long enough, and given me disaster for a dowry."

I caught my breath and waited for my blood to cool. I wanted him to look at me again, to show some sign of friendship, but he just stared out to sea.

"And what will become of you, who departed untrothed and spent your best years in foreign lands? When our princes roamed the women's tents and divided up the spoils, did they think of a wife for loyal Elpenor—did they think of that? It's shameful!"

I tried to say more, but he raised his hand to silence me. The wind stirred and the air smelled of sparks, like the start of a gale. We heard the voice of the goddess then, singing from some inner chamber.

The first note was a splash of molten gold. Transmuted by the heat of her song, it flared into an argent shimmering, like a shoal of skipjacks rippling beneath the breakers. Suddenly, it burst into the shining clash of cooled bronze. Stunned with pious dread, we were too afraid even to cover our ears. Men, we were sure, were not meant to hear this song.

Panicked, I tried to summon the sound of human music, to call back the days spent at my mother's feet, staring up while she chanted the old hymns and sent the spindle twirling from her thigh. But then a flush of crimson struck my eyes, unfurling in a pulsing bloom. The voice blanched, flattened to a luminous disc that burned with the fenny glow of sunless caves. Kirke's final notes fell in a shower of cinders that winked and then blackened against the sable sky. We were still for a long time after, listening to the flickering of the torches and the steady lashing of the surf.

"A song of parting."

"Yes," I said when I could speak again. "She must be releasing him." I wiped the wetness from my eyes. "What else could it mean? She must have shown him the way home!" Filled with joy, I crouched down and seized him by the shoulders. But he shook me off and turned away.

"Make haste, we have to tell the others."

"I'm not going."

"Elpenor," I said, "don't be stubborn. I was angry before. Let's be friends again and together we'll bear this good news back." I peered down into the courtyard. The proud panther had wandered off, preferring a bed of pine needles to one of stone.

"I'll stay a bit longer," he said. "The night is cool."

I opened my mouth to protest, but there was a familiar strangeness to his look. I had seen it once before, on the face of a dying soldier. On the field that day, what I'd seen, it wasn't the ecstasy of the stab, not the ravishing surge that follows. That was common enough. No, that kill had been different. As I drew my sword from the Trojan's ruined trunk, something had passed between us. He must have known the wound was mortal, and for a moment he seemed to be asking me to grieve with him for the life that was rushing away. I'd wanted to hearten him—his was a fine death; he had fallen defending the land of his fathers—but the words had stuck in my throat. He'd dropped away from me then and fell, gaping, into a well of darkness.

On the roof, I stared, uncomprehending, into Elpenor's face. He seemed to smile, then turned away, seaward, to gaze down the darkened path that led to shore.

Back in the hall, swaddled in thick pelts, I slept until the captain came to wake me. He went the same to each man, bidding us to return to the ship. The men were in high spirits as we boarded. Some sang, others wept openly. When we took our places along the thwart, no one asked after the empty seat. I thought of Elpenor, probably dozing on the roof, but said nothing. Let the boy dream away in sweet sleep, I thought. Let him stay and forget if he can.

Alone among the crew, I witnessed the goddess, heavy with child, lead a ram and a black ewe aboard ship. Then the sails unfurled and that reckless man swung the prow of our black ship north, toward the house of Hades. The two beasts, tethered fast to the mast pole, turned to face the dawn. With bright, dumb eyes, they looked out over the reddening sea.

The Master of Sleep

THERE WAS ONCE a man in our town who could sleep longer, more deeply, and more beautifully than anyone else. Not a native of this place, Don Albani appeared one morning at the bridge that spans the Esarulo, a little river that bounds our parish at its western edge. Seen from our ramparts, he seemed less a man than a bare and twisted tree sprung up from the stones of the old viaduct. Three times we spied him at an arch's crest, pausing for reasons known only to himself, before descending again into the fog that swaddled the bridge. We might have mistaken him for a trick of the mists had he not manifested at our gate and, making use of the lion-faced knocker, made his presence known in all its solidity.

Once inside, he crossed the piazza and proceeded directly to the office of the municipal clerk. There the stranger declared himself the sole living descendant of the Albani (an illustrious name not spoken in these parts for generations) and therefore due by hereditary right to some land hereabouts. Possessed of documents substantiating both his crest and claim, signor Arturo degli Albani took possession that very day of the chestnut orchards and the lowland cottage that comprised his patrimony.

At first, the Don didn't mix much with us, taking apertivo at the inn perhaps one evening out of twenty, staying only long enough to fortify himself with a few olives, a slice or two of salted tomato, and a glass of red vermouth. His head was crowned with soft ivory curls, and he smelled of rosewater and fresh wood shavings. He was rangy, with a long sharp face, but his gauntness suggested more the self-denial of an anchorite than the privation of a beggar. His clothes were rumpled, though finely made, and he often adorned his jacket with a red poppy (only slightly wilted). On those few occasions when he lifted his glass to join us in a toast, one of his sleeves would draw back from the wrist to reveal a lacy cuff.

It was obvious that the Don had once been a person of some distinction, but it was not until the first seekers arrived that we learned of his fame in the courts and great cities of the country. Hollow-eyed men afflicted by the eternal wakefulness of insomnium gathered like shades in the corners of the inn, the rawboned fellows brooding over glasses of warm milk but never renting a bed. Soon others followed: men who snorted and grunted like horses, sleepers seized by fevers who drenched their bedclothes, hysterics who screamed and thrashed through the night—all these and more came to seek the counsel of that venerable gentleman, honoring his name with the epithet "the master of sleep."

We learned from these supplicants that the good old man had, in his day, been the foremost practitioner of the somnolent arts. He possessed knowledge of every growing thing and could, from raw and unfinished nature, distill oils and tinctures with the power to dampen an ardent spirit or transmute the base lead of torpor into the lustrous gold of vigilance.

But the maestro's reputation was not founded on such incidental pursuits. The people had reserved their highest praise for one of his talents in particular: his ability to fall, instantly and at will, into a voluptuous sleep from which he could not be roused until the precise moment of his choosing. Before the art of sleep fell out of fashion at court, his performances had been staged in a canopied bed in the most illustrious hall of the palace, always drawing a great crowd. He was thought to be very handsome then, and more than a few of the unmarried ladies in the capital (and some of the married ones, too) were known to keep miniature portraits of the artist concealed in their dressing tables. A countess, famous for her boldness, was said to possess a locket containing a golden curl snipped from the sleeper's tousled head.

Later, when the identity of the old Don was widely known in our region, it became troublesome for him to receive so many visitors in his modest cottage. So, gracious man that he was, he agreed to make himself available for counsel at the inn on the evening of each new moon. Arrangements were made, and a corner table in the common room was set aside for his use. To preserve the discreet character of his consultations, the Don himself provided an oriental screen consisting of panels of mulberry paper framed by slats of lacquered cherry. The lamp set between physician and patient projected their outlines onto the screen, transforming each encounter into a shadow play.

Despite his good works and the prestige he brought to our town, the maestro's presence among us was not without controversy. Some whispered that the ingenious old man must be a witch, his great knowledge an infernal boon granted by Lucifer to his staunchest servant. A few said openly that the Don was no different than that gravedigger from Magasa, the one who had come through town with a sack of paupers' bones, passing them off as true relics of the saints. These men swore, one to the other, that if this proud fellow proved to be a charlatan, he could expect the same treatment as the other: a shorn head, a shirt of pitch and feathers, and a ride through town on a post.

But there was one, Baldo the printer's son, who resented the Don's celebrity more than all the others. Just as the inked impression is backward to the block that makes it, so Baldo's nature was in perfect contradiction to that of his gentle and fastidious father. The printer had been a widower and too tenderhearted to beat the boy, and so with no mother and no blows to correct him, the wicked child had gone about doing whatever he pleased: chasing girls with fresh-cut switches, setting dogs' tails on fire, and forcing his will on the younger boys. Never learning to read himself, the son scorned his father's trade. When he came of age, he left our town and entered into the service of a condottiero, one of those disreputable princes whose banner can be bought with gold.

It was a few weeks after the Don's arrival when the prodigal returned from his years of soldiering. He asked after his father, and it was with heavy hearts that we told him of the good man's fate. The previous winter, the old printer had been shaken with a fierce ague and, after three days, had returned to the One who had formed him from the dust. Upon hearing this news, Baldo displayed no signs of anguish but instead set to carousing at the inn, drinking all through the days and evenings and telling stories of his exploits to any who would listen. He was still there when, on the appointed night, Don Albani arrived with his screen. A reverential quiet settled over the common room, broken only when Baldo asked who this old man could be and why everyone paid him such deference.

Informed of the Don's mastery of the art of sleep, Baldo crumpled his swinish face and one of his ears—the tip of which had been mangled in some battle and was now clipped like that of a fighting dog—flushed red and twitched.

"Any man can sleep," he claimed; there was no special science to it. Once, he boasted, after a five-day forced march through the marshes, he'd collapsed on the damp ground and slept straight through a cavalry charge. He began to relate more of the story, but no one minded him. The Don was seated with his first client and all eyes turned to watch the shadowy spectacle. Seething with rage, Baldo waited until the Don had concluded his first interview before crossing the room and rapping on the screen.

"My good sir," the Don said, stepping from behind his paper shield, "I'm afraid I can't see you now, as several are already waiting. But if you will write your name and the nature of your malady in the ledger there—"

At the mention of writing, Baldo bristled. "What I need from you—and right here and now—is satisfaction for this itch I have." He leaned in close and seized the maestro by the forelock. "It's my nose, you see. Whenever it comes near a liar, or a cheat, or a rascal, it begins to itch and to vex me." He pressed a fistful of snowy curls to his face. His nose—a ruddy thing overlaid with a skein of broken veins—flared and snuffled like a hog's. "Just as I reckoned," he said, releasing his grip, "you've got the stink of a swindler on you." Leaning back, Baldo folded his arms across his chest. "You're no kind of master, you old crow, not of any honest craft." Those present raised up a cry, appalled to see the good man so abused. But, languidly lifting his arm, the Don bade us to be silent.

"The drunkard's insult must sometimes be endured," he said, smoothing his hair back to its natural shape, "for he does not know what he does and may beg forgiveness when the spell passes." The Don then brought one hand to his breast and unhooked the blossom fastened there. "Yet the dictates of my order do not allow for indulgence in a case such as this. You have insulted my honor—which, in itself, is of little consequence. But you have committed another, graver offense. You have impugned the eternal verity of the Stygian arts. And that, sir, must be answered." The poppy fell in a slow spiral, turning three times before landing on the toe of Baldo's boot. The brute furrowed his brow, then bent to retrieve the flower.

"Ah," the Don said, "so you accept my challenge. All the worse for you."

"You? Against me? I'd break you over my knee like a bundle of dried sticks."

"And so forfeit the trial by slumber by laying hands on your adversary? That's no strategy, friend."

"A trial? What are you on about?"

"A contest, one with a storied history among the members of my order. Each of us shall lie flat on our backs and, as soon as we are able, allow sleep to overtake our senses. The first man to wake concedes defeat."

"I'd just as soon drag you out by your ear and dash your skull against the cobbles."

"But what would that prove?" posed the Don. "The question is not of your strength, but of my art. If, as you say, I am a fraud, what could you possibly have to fear from such a contest? Weren't you saying before, if I heard you correctly, that you could sleep even in the midst of a battle?"

Baldo turned his head this way and that, looking into our expectant faces. He would not yield to the old man, but dragging him into the street and thrashing him now would seem unsportsmanlike. The Don, it appeared, had lured him into a trap, one Baldo did not have the wits to disarm.

"Fine, then," he said. "But I'll have your word. If I show you to be a faker, you'll take your tricks and leave this place."

"Agreed," the Don said, a smile creeping across his face. He then clapped his hands and ordered two long tables to be cleared and set side-by-side in the center of the room. At his direction, sheets were brought down from the upper chambers and spread over each.

These modest accommodations in place, the Don explained the terms of the contest. The challenge would begin when both men were so deeply asleep that the sound of an empty pot struck with a ladle could not rouse them. Following the successful performance of this test, the first to wake, whether minutes later or after many days, would forfeit the contest. The particulars of the trial were left for us to determine, and volunteers presented themselves to stand watch in shifts.

The competitors took their places and closed their eyes. A change came over the master the moment he entered into his trance. Like a sea becalmed, his face became placid, the lines of age smoothing to such a degree that he appeared to regain the freshness of youth. Oh that smile, blameless and beatific, and yet there was something sphinxlike in it.

What unaccustomed pleasures did he relish? What forbidden desires could not be indulged by one who could master dreams? Or might he choose not to dream at all, preferring instead to abide in the marrow of silence, beyond the reach of any hardship?

On the second night, it was discovered that Baldo talked in his sleep. He complained about his rations, cursed his captains and his horse, and several times whimpered pitifully for the mother who had died to give him breath. As the night deepened, Baldo's groaning grew louder and more guttural until, just as the cock crowed on the morning of the third day, he sat upright and howled. Crazed and trembling, he leapt from the table.

"Did you see it?" he demanded, gripping the watchman by the shoulders and shaking him awake. "The ghost!" Baldo had been visited by an apparition, a perfect likeness of his father down to the thick moustache and the blue-black stains beneath his fingernails. In one of its bloodless hands, the shade had held out a composing stick. With the other, it delved into the pockets of a leather apron, drawing out strips and blocks of lead. It seemed to know the pieces it sought by touch alone, for it kept its gaze fixed on Baldo as it placed one letter after another into the stick.

Baldo petitioned the ghost to state its purpose and disclose its origin—whether it had fallen from Heaven's celestial sphere or fled the caverns of the damned through some vent in the earth. But the phantom would not speak. Instead, it held the composing stick before it, presenting a single line of type, now fully set. But unlettered as he was, Baldo could not read the message. A moment later, the shade had turned away and, sliced through by the first ray of dawn, scattered into so many motes of dust.

As for the Don, he continued sleeping peacefully. Looking closely at his countenance, however, some detected an arch to one eyebrow, a wily curl of the lip that belied the innocence of his smile. Once Baldo had steadied himself, he crouched next to the maestro's ear, addressing him in a loud voice.

"You've had your fun, you old witch. Putting a thing like that into a man's dreams—won't you and the devil have a good laugh the next time you meet?" The Don's chest rose and fell, but he said nothing. "And I'll grant you've got some craft after all, heathenish though it is. If it were up to me, you'd burn for it." Baldo took the wilted poppy, forgotten until now, out of his pocket. "But you can take your flower now and go back to your own house." He tossed the blossom onto the Don's chest, but still the master remained motionless.

Then, as if drawn upward by unseen strings, the Don's arms floated into the air. Seemingly without his knowing anything about it, his fingers made a series of exquisite gestures. We took their execution as a sign that the Don had entered into some new, elevated stage of meditation. It was clear now that he did not intend to wake until he had favored us with a prolonged demonstration of his art.

Many days passed and still the Don reposed in gorgeous sleep. By the middle of the second week, however, the lodgers had grown tired of carrying their boots down the stairs each morning and then lacing them up at the threshold. No longer a solemn, sock-footed procession, they returned to their former habit of tramping down the stairs in a throng, each man scrambling and shoving to be among the first to the breakfast table. The serving girl, who had once stepped so gingerly around the maestro's pallet, now bustled by with platters of food, knocking her ample hips against his bier-like bed.

There was a sense, even among those who had been its most ardent spectators, that the show had gone on too long. An odd compound of feelings stirred within us then, for our admiration of the old man's art was now adulterated with shame and no small portion of resentment. The infidelity of our attention, our deafness to the subtler registers of the maestro's instrument—these seemed to each citizen an indictment of his own coarse and uncultivated character.

Yet we took little time to ponder this change of sentiment, for it coincided with the end of the Lenten season, that time of the year in which every muscle and sinew of our communal body labors in preparations for the Holy Week. It is our custom, you see, for the several days that follow Palm Sunday to mount processions through the town, the execution of which requires the construction of stages and scaffolds, the decoration of wagons, the making of masks and costumes, the adornment of altars, and so on.

The festivities reach their climax on Maundy Thursday, with the reenactment of the last supper and the carrying of the cross. And we can hardly be blamed, given the pious drama of that spectacle, and followed as it was by the Easter Vigil and the feast celebrating our Lord's resurrection, for having attended so little to the old man asleep on his table. Nor did we think of him the Monday of the Easter market, that day when we open our gates to artisans and peddlers of all sorts.

In among that gathering of minstrels and moneylenders, of chandlers and cheesemongers, there was a young man calling himself Leandro. Attached to a troupe of comic actors, his performance was preceded by a Zanni in a long-nosed leather mask, a cunning servant who sported with a hunchbacked Pantalone. When this pair had finished, the dashing youth capered up the crates that served as steps and stood alone on the makeshift stage.

His face was comely and fresh, with no inkling of a beard. His hair, tawny-gold, was short and curled, the better to display his long forehead and high, delicate eyebrows. The lips of his small mouth were full, and when these parted, as in a smile, they disclosed a fetching gap between his front teeth.

Though his manner of dress may have been à la mode among the Florentines, it seemed to us fantastic. His doublet, myrtle green, had been slashed near to tatters—not thoughtlessly, we saw, but by design—so that puffs of lemon chemise protruded through the slits. Where our jackets were loose and reached as far as the knees, the boy's was short-waisted and fit him closely, not unlike a maiden's corset. This showed his slender figure to advantage and provided full view of his legs, long and shapely in pleatless hose. To cover his sinful parts he wore a padded pouch, of which modesty prevents me saying any more.

His arms quiet and trunk perfectly erect, Leandro lifted one foot to the level of his knee and with his pointed toes traced perfect circles in the air, all the while keeping to the tambourine's cheerful measure. This was no country circle dance of the kind all but the lame can perform, but something artful and athletic. His feet moved with complex intentions over the boards, and he pivoted into profile, placing one hand on his hip and gazing coyly over a raised shoulder before leaping straight up, crossing his feet twice at the ankles, and landing in the same stance as before. The end of his performance consisted of a vigorous series of turns—all performed while suspended in the air—concluding with a high kick.

It was the most remarkable display we had ever seen and, compelled by our cries of acclaim, he repeated his dance twice more before we allowed him to leave the stage. That evening we plied him with wine and extracted a promise that he would stay with us for at least a fortnight. He was reluctant at first, for he already had engagements with the actors in other places, but, he supposed, he could use the time to finish work on his book, a treatise on the art of dance that would codify his techniques and secure for him a reputation above even that of Domenico da Piacenza and Guglielmo the Hebrew. At the mention of a book, Baldo—quite drunk and expressing a manly affection for the boy—offered the use of his father's press (not mentioning, in his enthusiasm, that he knew nothing of its operations).

And that is how Leandro came to pass the spring with us and become our dancing master. In the mornings he practiced his footwork, retiring to his room in the afternoons to work at his manuscript. So great was his devotion to his art that in the evenings he offered lessons in courtly dancing to any who showed an interest.

After the evening meal, all of the benches and tables were placed against the walls. The table bearing Don Albani was moved from its regular place and wedged in the farthest corner. As we prepared the space for the first of these lessons, Leandro asked after our slumbering gentleman. Was the man always thus? He had known of such unfortunates in Venice. It was tragic to see an ancient fellow drink himself insensate night after night; were there no family or friends to look after him, to spare him this last disgrace in his declining years?

Oh no, we assured him, this was no drunkard, but a master of the art of sleep. The youth seemed not to understand. In his career as a dancing prodigy, he had served in several courts yet never once heard of a sleeping master. He admitted, however, that among the highborn, trends caught fire and were snuffed out with such celerity that the whole craze for sleeping could have passed before he was born. The boy looked the Don up and down, but then shrugged, appearing to put the matter out of his mind.

On that night and those that followed, Leandro divided us into pairs and showed us a new way of dancing. We learned to greet our partners with a single step forward and back—with the left foot and taking care not to point the toe or drag the heel. This was followed by a bending of both knees, a sort of bow, but with a straight back and arms at our sides. Although it made us feel foolish at first, we even became willing to mime the kissing of our fingers before commencing each dance.

There were so many steps to learn, to which our young master kept adding new ones. He led us through muffled walking steps and loud, cracking stamps of heel and toe. There were steps in which we circled one another and others where we sprung to the side or made a turn; another required the dancer to hop on one foot and swing the other like the clapper of a bell. The youth was very patient with us, even when we stumbled into each other or fell to the ground after a too-ambitious jump. There were only minor injuries and everyone agreed it was a fine time.

Not only did these lessons fill our nights with gaiety, but they had other effects as well. Our wives and the young maidens of our town seemed more appealing than before, both more dignified and in better spirits. Likewise, the hidden nobility of each man was revealed by his display of courtly graces. Baldo especially was transformed. He drank less and took more care with his appearance and his words. It was as if he had been waiting his whole life for just this kind of instruction: to be shown, down to the smallest gesture, how he ought to behave around other people.

Things went on in this way for several weeks until, one night, as we practiced the greatest yet of Leandro's miming dances—an elaborately choreographed battle of the sexes—we heard a rasp from the corner where the Don had been installed. His eyes were half-open and he was laboring, with some difficulty it seemed, to sit up. Leandro put a stop to the dance and several of us rushed over to attend the old gentleman.

We helped the Don down from his table and onto a proper bench. In a quiet voice, he bade us bring him a glass of water and a bowl of broth. When these were delivered, he took a sip of each and then asked for the date. He seemed pleased with our answers and nodded, allowing himself a self-satisfied smile at his achievement. It was only then that he inquired about the state of the common room. We had needed to move his table with the others, we explained, in order to make room for the dancing. He looked around, appearing to take in everything, after which he stared down into his bowl and set to eating his soup.

There was nothing to do but return to the dance. Leandro hurried us through the middle section of his "Gamomachia"—he had not yet completed the ending—and then, as was his habit on these nights, took up the lute himself and provided us with tunes fit for the slow and stately Padovane, rising in crescendo to the quick-stepping Gagliarda. Such a long sleep seemed to have dulled the Don's senses and left him weak. He watched us with sunken eyes, and though we encouraged him to join us, he dismissed the idea with a wave of his hand.

But then, for the last dance, he rose unsteadily to his feet and tottered to the edge of our circle. Out of consideration for the old man, Leandro played a soft, down-tempo number. We each sought out our usual partners. The Don bowed to an imaginary lady, and, watching us out of the corner of one eye, tried a few steps. His efforts were competent and though he smiled in wan imitation of our joy, gladness seemed not to touch him.

When the music was finished, while everyone was setting the room for the next day, I brought the Don his folded screen.

"I will go now," he said. "But it is late and I am weary from my performance. Would you be so kind as to walk with me?"

I said I would be honored and helped the old man to his feet. Together we proceeded to the town's smaller, eastern gate, and then onto the darkened path that led to the maestro's grove of chestnut trees. At the door to his cottage he hesitated.

"All of this," he said, sweeping his arm in a gesture that seemed to encompass the orchard and the town, the river and the mountains, the sky above us and all the stars. "This splendor. I never knew what to do with it, what it was for." He stared at my face as if he expected to find an answer there, but in truth I could not understand him. "Better to go inside and sleep." He took his screen from me and went inside the house. As I turned to leave, I heard the clatter of a key in the lock.

All this happened years ago, and the grass has grown wild again over the graves of the Albani, and the foundation of the cottage has failed and sunk half into the ground. Yet we have not seen the Don since that night and, as far as any of us know, he sleeps there still.

A Hungry Ghost

I WAS OUTSIDE Frank's Kitchen, smoking the last of a cigarette that had ended up in my hand, when I saw the hungry ghost. That patch of sidewalk, the place where people smoked, it overlooked the entryway to a basement apartment. No one had lived there for a long time, but there was still that corridor, just below the level of the street. I tossed my cigarette, watched as it traced a sizzling arc into the trench.

The shadows below seemed to ripple, and I caught glimpses of a hunched, shambling thing. A bare head. An enormous abdomen suspended on a pair of spindly legs. The creature's skin was waxen and pearlescent, stained shades of blue by the twilight. It worked feverishly, tearing away filters, seizing and unwrapping the singed stubs of rolling papers. With a long, swollen tongue, it lapped at flakes of tobacco, its throat making a sodden, choking sound.

I recognized it for what it was: a yidag. In a previous life, it had been a human being, one so consumed by craving and desire that after death it was condemned to wander the earth, tormented always by a gnawing pain, as if its belly were host to a swarm of biting insects. The taste in my mouth—so suddenly bitter—caused me to retch. The creature twitched, swung its head upward, and I found myself staring down into its bloated face. Its tiny, puckered mouth expressed nothing, but its eyes were anguished. A thing rotted through with regret.

I backed away, tried to take slow, even breaths, to recall the few tantric practices I knew, the ones for calming fear and generating loving-kindness. But my mind was paralyzed. I may study the lives of the great yogis, but I'm no Padmasambhava, no tamer of demons. I turned and ran. Pushing open the door to Frank's, I mounted the stairs two at a time until I reached the bar on the second floor.

Inside, things were just as I'd left them. My drink was sitting on the bar, the ice melting. Lindsay was pouring shots of cinnamon-flavored whiskey. I got back to my stool and ordered one.

"Russell, I thought you only drank gin."

"Expanding my horizons." My hand was trembling badly, and I spilled some of the stuff getting it to my mouth. Lindsay didn't say anything. She swept a rag over the sticky spot on the bar and went back to stocking the cooler with beer.

The alcohol and the loud talk of the people at the bar, these began to soothe me. For a moment, I questioned whether I'd imagined the thing outside, if it was the booze playing tricks on me. I couldn't deny it—I'd been out on a tear the last few nights. Ever since I'd lost my job.

I'd been a short-timer at the university, grant-funded, my days spent in a too-bright room in the basement of the library, cataloging biographies of some Lamas from eastern Tibet, all of them long dead. I'd devoted twenty years to studying the Kagyu masters, their lives and works. Could I be starting to see the world as they did?

According to the Lamas, the world was full of spirits and incarnations. Most of us were just too wrapped up in the drama of our own suffering and desires to notice. How many yidags had I encountered before this, not knowing what they were? Dozens, maybe hundreds—on street corners and in parks late at night, in cheap bars and motels off the interstate. Wherever need and misery congealed. No doubt some of them looked like ordinary people, at least some of the time; others might not know they were yidags at all.

I'd been drinking, but the thing in that pit was no hallucination. It had as much claim on reality as anyone else at Frank's. As real as Lindsay with her tattooed knuckles and her smoker's cough, or Mitch, in his weight-lifting shirt, standing sentry at the end of the bar, leaving his post only to play one of three heavy metal songs on the jukebox. I squinted at the other people in the bar, half believing I could pierce through their disguises. But they all looked the same.

"Are you all right?" Lindsay asked.

"Yeah, sure," I said, embarrassed. "Can I get another G&T?" I glanced up at the televisions above the bar. One was showing an action movie with the sound turned off, its car chases and fist fights made more insipid by the closed captions: [grunting], [police siren wailing], [bones crunching]. On the other screen, a pack of long sleek dogs chased a mechanical hare.

Frank's Kitchen had been my regular spot since moving to the city. Downstairs, Frank's was a family place more or less, a greasy spoon with a black-and-white checkered floor. Upstairs, though, it was a dive bar favored by low-end hipsters, high-functioning alcoholics, and off-duty cooks and servers. There were booths set along the outer walls, a dance floor that could be cleared of chairs and tables to accommodate a band (usually metal or punk rock), and a unisex bathroom with three filthy stalls.

Plenty of people—not just the tourists, but regular diners, too—either didn't know there was an upstairs or didn't care to find out. In the beginning, this had been what appealed to me. I could do my work during the day and, when it was done, climb those narrow steps to a place where I could be certain never to encounter anyone from my life outside. At the bar, on a wooden stool upholstered in black vinyl,

I could drink with my own kind. I hadn't been making much at the university—not after the credit card companies and the student loan people took their share—and Frank's had just about the cheapest drinks in town. Besides, they knew me there. More than once, Lindsay leaving a few drinks off my tab had made the difference between paying a bill and not paying it.

Few of the stools were occupied at this hour, and almost all by men. I took this as a bad sign, an omen of an unlucky night. I preferred talking to women, striking up associations that gave a nice glow to things all the way through to last call. At closing time, we'd say our goodbyes, sometimes exchanging numbers and sometimes not.

I looked over my shoulder, hoping that one of these women might come up the stairs at just that instant and relieve me of my privacy. Instead, I saw Misty. She wore a thin jacket, the black vinyl crinkled like crepe paper, together with a pair of stone-washed jeans, the kind that, thirty years ago, had been favored by the popular girls in my high school.

"Look out," Lindsay said, refilling my drink, "it's the meth witch." I took another look, but there was nothing unusual about the woman. Her hair, bone black, was shaved at the back and sides, the thicker fringe arranged so that it swept across her forehead. She didn't have the sweaty, jangly energy of a meth head, and there were no scratch marks or scabs on her face.

Misty noticed my looking and her mouth seemed to break apart. A shameless smile, displaying the ruined teeth of her upper jaw. Quickly, as if I hadn't really been looking, I turned back to my drink. But Misty was already pulling out the stool next to mine. She ordered a beer and a shot of whiskey.

"Did you play this?" she asked, pointing her thumb at the jukebox.

"No, not me. That was someone else."

She had an ordinary face. It was not pretty, but there was nothing wrong with it either, no discernible defect—a cleft lip, say, or a wandering eye. Yet there was something about her features, unremarkable in themselves, that together produced an impression of homeliness.

I thought immediately of how I might get rid of her. I didn't like the idea of other people at Frank's thinking I was associated with this woman: her bad teeth and cheap clothes, her need for a stranger's attention. But then I caught myself, the way I might notice in meditation that I'd lost track of my breathing. A verse of the Bodhisattva vow came back to me, words I'd repeated so often and earnestly as a younger man: *So will I, too, for the sake of all beings, generate the mind of enlightenment.* The dreamy extravagance of my devotion in those days, my ludicrous self-importance, worn like the armor of an errant knight—it made me cringe to recall it.

Still, all those years spent studying sutras, of sitting with my ass on a meditation cushion, imagining I was breathing in the pain and suffering of all living beings, sending them relief and joy with each exhalation. What had it all been for, I wondered, if I couldn't bring myself, here and now, to be kind to a lonely woman in a bar, a harmless person who just wanted a little company?

"Did you hear something you liked?" I asked.

"'Jockey Full of Bourbon.' I've always loved Tom Waits."

I shared my theory that Waits had stolen his signature growl from Louis Armstrong.

"I don't know about that," she said, pausing to take her shot. "You've got to give Howlin' Wolf his due. And Waits's early stuff, he's leaning hard on Mississippi John Hurt."

That started us talking about music, which went on for maybe forty minutes before she told me her name and I told her mine. I was grateful for the distraction, anything to take my mind off the creature outside: its neck, a narrow ribbon of gristle, and—worst of all—that mouth, an obscene ring of muscle. Trying to put it out of my mind, I asked Misty about her work.

It turned out that for most of her life she'd been an office manager for a shipping company. But then her supervisor retired. The new boss didn't like her, made work so hellish that she had to quit. Since then, she'd been able to put together enough work to get by. Most of the week, she worked as a picker at an Amazon warehouse.

"I've got another job, cooking at a homeless shelter. Big industrial kitchen. It's mac and cheese, rice and beans, pizza. But at least with that one, I feel like I'm doing something that matters."

"I'm a translator," I offered. "Tibetan, a little Chinese."

"Huh. Are there a lot of Tibetans around here? I mean, there's that restaurant . . . "

"No, not like that. I work with texts, not people. Not a lot of people can read Tibetan, so I can usually find work at universities and libraries."

"You didn't want to be a professor?"

"I did, actually. Came pretty close. Only the dissertation left, but then I had a crack-up and had to drop out."

"Really? What was it about?"

She meant the breakdown, but I wasn't going to get into that. "Oh, saints mostly. Tibetan ones. A bunch of louts and scoundrels, really, at least the lineage I studied. Eventually, though, they each found their way to enlightenment. Hope for all of us, I guess."

I told her a little about Tilopa, who'd gotten his start as a solicitor for a prostitute, and Marpa the Translator, a bull of a man who put away pitchers of barley beer and flew into violent rages. I was beginning to enjoy myself. I didn't teach, so an opportunity to make a show of my learning was a rare and welcome thing.

"Were there any women saints?"

"Not in the Karma Kamtsang line. Sure, the black hats pay lip service to Yeshe Tsogyal, Niguma, Machig Labdrön—but none of those are direct lineage-holders." I knew these names meant nothing to her, but it pleased me to say them. An old feeling, usually suppressed, was welling up: a schoolboy's pride at knowing how to pronounce exotic, foreign words. "There are a few women in some of the other lines, but it's rare. You've got to understand, they were coming from a place culturally where being incarnated as a woman was considered a result of bad karma. *Kye men*, the Tibetan word for 'woman'? It literally means 'low born.'"

"Figures. Here and now, it's not so different." She tapped a pair of cigarettes from her pack, held them out, and flashed the same ghoulish smile as before. Those teeth. Beggar teeth, bag lady teeth. Nothing like rich teeth, which were smooth and gleaming and straight, their roots sheathed in pink gums that never bled. I'd grown up in the backwoods of Wisconsin and, before escaping to college, I'd known plenty of farmers and fishermen (and their wives and kids) who'd suffered with mouths full of cracked and broken teeth. I'd learned early: the further you fell from the ideal of rich teeth, the worse people treated you. Misty, I suspected, was treated worse than most.

"Well, do you want one or not?"

I wanted to decline, to stay indoors and away from the yidag. I was about to make an excuse, but then reminded myself that in all the literature, I'd never read an account of a yidag attacking a living person. Some hungered for human flesh, but only that of corpses. However repulsive its appearance, a hungry ghost was no wrathful deity, no blood-drinker. A yidag was a confused creature trapped between worlds, no more dangerous than a homeless man on a park bench, muttering into his matted beard. I followed Misty down the stairs.

Outside, the sun had set, and I strained to see into the trench. Nothing but trash and the muted shadows cast by the streetlamp. She held out a lighter and I leaned forward, sucking at the filter. A menthol, it left a cold chlorine taste in the back of my throat. A skittering noise came from the pit and she seized my arm.

"Oh, gross!" A blur of damp fur scurried across a railing, dropped to the sidewalk, and retreated into the alley. We moved off a few paces to stand under Frank's faded green awning. Shaken, I was taking deep drags, one after another, trying to finish quickly and get back inside.

"Take it easy," she said as I broke into a coughing fit. "You can have another. I've got plenty." My eyes began to sting and I bent over, hands on my thighs.

"You all right, honey?" She put her palm flat between my shoulder blades, stroked my back with slow tender circles until I could stand. It gave me a strange feeling. As if, in another incarnation, she'd been my mother, and I'd been her son. I know how it sounds. But over countless lives, didn't we all end up being each other's parents and children, husbands and wives, abusers and victims, living out all the possible combinations not just once but thousands of times?

When we got back to the bar, I bought her a drink. Lindsay looked wary and vaguely disgusted, and I wondered what she might know about Misty that I didn't.

"That's a nice ring," Misty said. "Someone at home waiting for you?"

"No, nobody. I'm divorced." The ring was titanium, with two bars of black ceramic, an equals sign. An unconventional wedding ring, Joanne and I had picked it out together. We'd loved each other, but after a while, my drinking became a problem. Then she met Louise. As their relationship deepened, ours began to make less and less sense. The divorce had been swift and uncomplicated; there'd been no children and little property. Our betrayals had been small, forgivable. I still liked wearing the ring. Most mornings I remembered to put it on the right hand, not the left.

"I was married once, too," Misty said. "He tried to be a good man, but he was too much his father's son. It's just me now, and sometimes my boy.

"He doesn't live with me, though," she added, as if to reassure me. Maybe she sensed the change in my attitude or maybe it was the booze, but she was more forward than before. One of her hands kept brushing against my thigh. At first, since no one could see, I decided to let it go. After a while, though, I had to say something.

"Look, I feel like I should tell you, I don't think tonight is going to turn out the way you want." She withdrew her hand. Her expression, which had been playful and eager to please, changed completely. It was as if she had peeled off the mask of her face, folding the membrane and placing it in her bag for later use. The thing underneath was deprived and grim, with no trace of hope in it at all.

"I've got a hotel room," she said flatly, staring into the mirror above the bar. "And I want to use it."

From behind, a hand gripped my shoulder and squeezed. It was Ed Vermilion, a tall hairless kid who favored orange-tinted aviators and loud, patterned shirts. Weeknights, he went from bar to bar in the square, selling cannabis candy and liquid THC. I was aware of Misty, her hopelessness forgotten, looking now at Ed.

"Hey, Russ. You make it home okay?"

"Last night? Yeah, sure." I'd been in a blackout, and whatever had happened that night, at least after midnight, I didn't remember it. In the morning, I'd found myself in bed, still in my clothes.

"The way you were running down that alley, I thought the cops must be after you."

At the back of my skull, I could feel a shudder of memory, the ungentle pressure of something pushing its way to the surface. The bathroom at Frank's, the yidag—was that the first time I'd seen it?—its face, inches from my own, yet somehow indistinct.

A noise—the crack and rattle of Lindsay slamming the cash drawer into place. As she approached, Ed stiffened. The week before, he'd been waving around an antique revolver he'd bought at an estate sale. Lindsay had thrown him out. Now he reached into his pocket and drew out a handful of hard candies, each one wrapped in brightly colored wax paper, like taffy from a county fair. He slid them across the bar. Lindsay sighed, pocketed them, and poured out a double shot of Jägermeister. All, it seemed, had been forgiven. Grinning, Ed patted me on the back and left to tend to his regular customers.

"Russell," Misty said once Lindsay was out of earshot. "Be honest. You're telling me you don't want to get laid tonight?"

Were there prostitutes who rented hotel rooms and then went to dive bars and spent two hours talking to a potential john before making a move? It didn't seem likely. I looked up from my drink, stared back at her, and shook my head.

"Well, I don't believe you. You do. Just not with me. So what's wrong with me anyway?"

"Jesus. You can't ask someone that."

"Why not? Come on, you can tell me."

I was embarrassed for her, a grown woman who thought another adult would ever answer that question truthfully. Then I remembered how often, over the years, I'd wanted to ask the same thing, of the friends who avoided me, the lovers who departed with flimsy explanations or no explanations at all, the strangers and acquaintances I formed attachments to and who felt nothing for me in return.

"I know I don't have the best face in the world," Misty offered. "But my work, it's very physical. I've got a great body."

It was true. As we'd headed up the stairs after smoking, I'd watched her ass, its shape like the round-bowled back of a mandolin. I'd been surprised at the sudden twinge of lust; my libido, keen and piercing when I was young, had been worn down to a dull nub by years of depression and medication. After an awkward silence, Misty graciously allowed me to change the subject to her work in the warehouse.

I imagined the place as a cavernous concrete cube fitted with rows of high white shelves, each containing bins of clear plastic, and inside each bin, a Surrealist's dream—the ears of a plush rabbit tangled in the tines of an electric egg beater, a pair of leopard-print ballet flats nestled against a Dover Thrift edition of *The Waste Land*.

"They use robots, right?"

"Not where I work. We do all the lifting. There are metal detectors, though. You have to go through one every time you leave the floor. And at lunch, when they ring the buzzer, there's a line. Of course they make you clock out first—they're not paying you to stand in line. So by the time you're through the machine and get your lunch—you can't bring it with you because you can't have any personal belongings on the floor, not even your phone—well, by the time you get to it, you've only got like ten minutes left to eat."

As we drank and talked, something started to wake up inside me. Maybe she'd been right the whole time; maybe, after all, I had wanted to get laid that night. And besides, I liked this woman. What would be the harm in a little thrill, some comfort for us both. It would only be for one night.

I lost some time at the bar. When I came to the surface again, we were crossing the street. My arm was around Misty's waist.

"Did we pay the tab?"

"I told you already," she said, pushing us through a set of revolving doors. In the bright glare of the hotel lobby, I sobered up enough to realize what we must look like to the other guests. The room was filled with well-dressed people, some with name cards dangling from their necks. Instead of heading to the elevators, Misty swerved in the direction of the hotel bar. I clung tighter to her waist, guiding her away from a collision with a stuffed leather chair.

"You don't want to go to the room?" I asked.

"It's early—we've got time for a couple more." She was obviously wasted. I pulled her, as gently as I could manage, into an alcove, a left-over space once meant for pay phones. Misreading my intentions, she placed her hand on my backside, and then we were kissing. It felt natural enough, despite the taste of her mouth, which was strongly metallic. Not coppery like blood; more like aluminum.

Placing my hands on her shoulders, I held her a short distance away from me. I looked her up and down, like a parent inspecting a child before sending her off to school. Summoning what I hoped was a stern expression, I said, "Okay. But just one, all right? And we're bringing it up to the room. We can't seem too drunk," I explained, "or they won't serve us."

She nodded and straightened her shoulders. A sly, bashful grin spread across her face. We stepped back into the lobby with a new feeling of affinity. We were a secret team, a couple of bad kids pulling one over on the grown-ups.

The room was on the sixth floor, oddly shaped and much smaller than I expected, with a single queen bed and a television mounted in the corner. Misty drank greedily from her Manhattan and set the glass on the nightstand. We came together again, making out with our clothes on. She made loud, throaty noises as I rubbed her inside her pants. We undressed and climbed onto the bed.

. . .

What should I tell you about what happened next? What, I wonder, would you believe and what, in the end, would you think it meant?

I could tell you about how, in that little room, Misty allowed me to see her true self, how she transformed into a radiant khandroma, a dancer in the boundless expanse of emptiness. I could tell you about her fangs and five-skull crown; the furnace of heat radiating from her bare, sindoor skin; the jewelry fashioned from the bones of the charnel grounds—about how they clattered as she danced before me holding a long, hooked dagger. I could tell you how, after our coupling, she cut open her heart and showed me its inner vastness, containing the whole of the empty, unborn universe.

But this is not that kind of story, and I'm not that kind of man. I may study the lives of the great Lamas, but I'm not like them. The sky dancers don't initiate me into mysteries; they don't offer me their secret hearts.

Later, we lay in bed together, her body curled against mine. I ran my hand over the stubble at the back of her head, and she toyed with the thatch of white hair on my chest.

"When did you know?" she asked.

"Know what?"

"You really couldn't tell?" She scratched her fingernails playfully over the skin of my belly. "Oh, I get it, you're trying to be nice."

"I'm not."

Was she a sex worker after all? Did she imagine, having gone this far, I wouldn't object to fetching some cash from the ATM in the lobby? Or maybe she was ill, her symptoms well concealed. That was probably it. She was infected with something horrible and contagious.

"I'm homeless."

My hand kept stroking the back of her head. I tried to reconcile my idea of a homeless person with the woman in bed next to me. On closer inspection, I could see that her hair, though cut in a trendy style, had probably been done at home. That, in itself, gave nothing away; plenty of the punk girls cut each other's hair. And Misty was so clean.

Her naked body smelled like tea and lavender oil, and her legs and the flesh under her arms were smooth. Perhaps she'd rented the room as an indulgence, an opportunity to clean up and care for herself. The rental market in the city was brutal. I could imagine a scenario in which two jobs allowed her to splurge on a hotel room now and then, but didn't provide enough for a place of her own.

"Well?"

For the first time that night, I couldn't think of anything to say. She slid out from under my arm and turned on her side.

"Asshole," she said to the wall. "You think you're better. But you were alone at the bar, same as me, getting fucked-up at five o'clock."

"Hey. Come on. I didn't say—"

"Fuck off."

I waited for her to say more, but she was quiet.

"Maybe I should go."

"Forget it."

"I mean, I could . . ."

She reached back and draped my arm across her shoulders. "We're too drunk. Let's just sleep." After a while, her breathing slowed and she began murmuring something I couldn't understand.

I woke up to Misty snoring. She'd rolled onto her back and her mouth had fallen open, releasing a sour, ocean smell. I saw now that her teeth were not uniformly gray. Some were a milky, translucent white, others tawny brown or the shiny black of beetle shells. Her gums had receded, and some of the teeth looked improbably long. As she slept, I stared at one of her incisors: a naked, horrible fang.

She was what I'd left behind, might fall into, what I'd counted on education, a life of culture and study, to deliver me from. How precarious my own situation was: the daily drinking, the student loans I'd never pay back, the maxed-out credit cards. My position at the university, the one thing that had granted the life I'd been living a sheen of respectability, that was gone now, too. I could drink every night in a dive bar, occasionally fall in with the people I met there, but I wouldn't be spending the night in this hotel room, not with a homeless woman. That would mean something: that my life had finally, perhaps irretrievably, spun out of control. I crept out of bed, pulled on my clothes, and took the elevator to the lobby.

I wanted to be free again. At least according to this certain notion I had of freedom. A state of sovereign solitude. An ego of and from itself, shaping without being shaped. The most universal of delusions, the cause and condition of all our suffering.

But leaning into the revolving door, it was still what I wanted most, to pass into anonymity, cut clean from the problems of other people. As the mechanism turned, I looked forward to the slight sucking sound of air leaving the enclosure, the momentary imposition of my own private vacuum. The door spun slowly, one blade succeeding another until I was out on the street.

It was morning, though only just, the sun and moon still sharing the sky. I looked across the street, at Frank's and the pit. No sign of the yidag. I followed the sidewalk as it wound around the bars and bookshops, their windows dark, twice imagining I heard the slaps of bare feet against the damp concrete. Turning, finding nothing, I hurried on. Without seeing it, I could sense its presence, like an odor of stale smoke clinging to my clothes. A few blocks from the old burial grounds, its colonial gravestones inscribed with feathered skulls, there was a liquor store I knew. I turned the corner and said a prayer: *Please, let the doors be open.*

Ghost Bike

PERRY TOOK THE last tablet from the cylinder clipped to his keys, placed it under his tongue, and waited for things to sort themselves out. Someone was on the phone, and then the airline people, a buzzing cloud of reprimands and false courtesy, hustled him on board and into his seat. He bit the pill in two, then worked at chewing it down to a fine powder. His mouth filled with a sour taste and he closed his eyes, waiting for his body and the earth below him to drop away.

He didn't remember landing or stepping off the plane, but his legs, it seemed, were carrying him through the terminal. A pair of automatic doors closed behind him and he entered a tunnel of roaring heat. He was aware of waiting in a line with others, but mostly he focused on the pleasure of scratching his bare forearms. A man, his skin the pale russet of river clay, took hold of Perry's bag and motioned for him to get in a cab.

As they merged onto the highway, a slow smile spread across Perry's face. It was like being a boy again. The sweet security of a family trip—curled in the back seat, feigning sleep and listening to his parents murmur in the dark.

"All right, all right," the driver said into his cell phone, "thirty minutes." He tossed the phone onto the passenger seat, slung one arm over the headrest, and turned in Perry's direction. "Strippers," he said, as if that explained everything. "Now, where am I taking you?"

"The Criminal Court," he said, "in Orleans Parish."

The driver nodded and turned back to the road. Perry rested his head against the window. Without prompting, the driver started talking about his job, nights running meals to working girls on Bourbon Street and then retrieving them from wherever they ended up in the morning. There was a mild music to his speech, and it was pleasant to listen to him talk. *A lullaby*, Perry thought, and closed his eyes.

"So, where are you coming from?"

"Des Moines," he said, blinking awake. A low iron fence ran parallel with the highway and beyond that a lawn he thought must be a golf course. But back from the road there were statues and white granite crosses. There were stone tombs with slanted roofs, little cottages for the dead.

"The court, huh?" the driver said, grinning into the rearview. "Let me guess, too much fun on your last visit?" Perry didn't answer. "Well, that's all right." They turned off the highway and onto a busy avenue.

"Not me," Perry said a while later. "It was my son. He was hit by a car." The driver looked puzzled, so he added, "I'm here for the body." It seemed strange to say "the body" instead of "his body," as if it were a thing that had ceased to belong to Morgan. A stupid thought—the problem wasn't one of belonging. There wasn't a Morgan for things to belong to anymore.

"Lord, that's hard." The man shook his head back and forth. "You have any people here?"

"People? No." The car stopped, and the driver reached back and handed him a card. "I'm Charles. While you're here, you call me, wherever you are, and I can be there in a half hour, forty-five minutes." Perry paid the fare and waited for his chance to cross the street.

In the courthouse lobby, two officers stood guard. The man was broad-chested with a straight back. He had the practiced, apologetic friendliness of a man who could break things. The woman sat on a narrow stool in front of an X-ray machine, smacking her gum. They pointed him toward a hallway, and at the bottom of the stairs, in the basement, he found a wooden door. ORLEANS PARISH CORONER'S OFFICE was painted in block letters across the glass panel, and a no-smoking sign hung over the letter slot, fixed there with a strip of masking tape.

There were more papers to fill out. He'd already arranged things with the funeral home in Des Moines, all the raw details. He'd been embarrassed when they'd asked about clothing from home. Morgan had left when he was sixteen, and whatever hadn't gone to Goodwill wasn't likely to fit him anymore.

He scanned the accident report, afraid to read it too carefully: "Saint Claude Avenue Bridge . . . nineteen-year-old man . . . struck from the back by a Dodge Caravan . . . ejected from the bike to the eastbound left travel lane . . . struck by a Chevy Avalanche . . . " He brought the papers to the woman behind the counter. Her nails, brightly painted and fixed with plastic stones, made a ticking sound against the clipboard. She went to the back and returned with a padded envelope. Perry put it in his luggage with the rest of his things.

"Do I . . . is now when I identify him?"

"No, baby," she said. He couldn't remember the last time a stranger had called him "baby." A throb of childish need moved through him. He wanted this woman to put her arms around him and pull him close, to coo and console him. He reached for his pill holder, forgetting for a moment that it was empty. Before he left, he'd locked his prescriptions in the shop safe, rationing only enough to get him through the flight. He didn't want to be medicated on this trip. He owed it to Morgan to feel something.

"Someone acquainted with the deceased," the woman said. "They already identified the body."

"Do you know who it was?"

The woman looked up, her face already set. Maybe it was the need in his eyes, he wasn't sure, but her expression softened. She glanced over her shoulder to see if anyone was watching, then wrote something on a slip of paper. She folded the note in half and handed it to him across the counter.

Outside, the sun shone fiercely. His mouth was dry and his scalp prickled with sweat. He followed the sidewalk past a flophouse and a used-car lot, then turned onto Canal Street and walked in the direction of the river. He'd expected palm trees, but the street was lined with live oaks. Their roots broke through the cement and spilled onto the sidewalk in tangled heaps. The shade was welcome, but for several blocks he had to give up on rolling his suitcase and carry it.

On the far side of the overpass, a roil of locals and tourists tumbled into each other: they shouted and slapped backs, waited for the bus with plastic bags from the pharmacy, spat on the sidewalk, scuffled, doubled over with laughter. On the boulevard, a police cruiser made a U-turn and bullied its way through the crush of traffic. Perry stopped in the midst of it all and stood there, astonished. All these people, what were they doing? Didn't they know his son had just died? It took an elbow jabbing him to bring him back to the world.

When he got to the hotel, he checked in at the desk and took the elevator to the sixth floor. In his room, he sat on the edge of the bed and took out his phone. There were five voice mail messages—all from Karen, of course. There was no point in listening. He could imagine them: Why had he insisted on going alone? Did he remember to claim his bags at the airport? He wasn't eating spicy food, was he? Was he eating at all? What kind of a man was he, abandoning his wife at a time like this? Did he think that because she hadn't given birth to Morgan that she didn't have a right to be there?

He stood up and retrieved the envelope from the coroner's office. There were a couple of cassette tapes inside, receipts from a local grocery, and some kind of homemade publication, photocopied and stapled, with typewritten rants about capitalism and gentrification. At the bottom, he found a ring of keys and a wallet with a few dollars in it. Handling Morgan's things, his chemical buffer against the world already spent, he braced for the force of his grief to crash over and crumple him. But he didn't feel anything, really—except that maybe there had been some slight adjustment to the laws of gravity. He sensed that if he took a step forward, he might rise off the floor and drift out the window. He lowered himself onto the bed again, lay back, and gently gripped the sides of the mattress.

The last time he'd seen Morgan, it had been after a late night at the shop. A mountain bike on the rack, Perry had chewed a pill and taken his time repairing a bent derailleur. That was something he'd always liked about the pills; he could take them and still work—for hours, in fact—concentrated and content. Well after the job was done, he stayed crouched next to the ten-speed, savoring the whisper of the spinning wheels, the finger-snap of the chain as it vaulted over the sprockets.

When he got home, he could hear Morgan and Karen arguing in the kitchen. Framed by the empty doorway, the scene looked like some old painting. There was a boy, his skinny arms stretched out and his face twisted in anguish. The big woman, fleshy and pink beneath her nightgown, leaned toward him. Comforter or tormentor, she could've fit either role in the picture.

"Everything is not fine," Morgan said. "It's totally screwed up." His voice splintered. "But you act like nothing's wrong. It's like you're a zombie—you're both zombies, and you're trying to make me one, too—like you want to eat my brains—" Karen let out a noise like a startled bird. "Don't laugh at me," Morgan said, pleading. "Why are you laughing?"

"I'm sorry," she said. She covered her mouth with her hand. "Of course, it's not funny. It's just the way you're talking."

Perry stepped into the light and reached between them. He took his dinner plate out of the refrigerator and carried it over to the counter.

"There you are," Karen said. "I must have called you six times."

"I was working."

"I don't know if you're interested, but your son was arrested tonight. The police brought him home in a squad car. The whole neighborhood must have seen it."

"But I didn't do anything."

Perry put his plate in the microwave and started it up.

"They found him in some boarded-up house in Drake. A party, with alcohol, if that was even the worst of it." Perry sighed and rubbed his eyes. Hunched in front of the microwave, he watched the slow turning of the plate. "How were you going to get home?"

"I was going to crash there. Lots of people do." He turned to see Morgan sweep his backpack off the table and onto his shoulder. "It's not like I'm wanted around here."

"You are not spending the night in a crack house."

"It's not a crack house."

"Let's everybody take it down a notch," Perry said.

Morgan stood there, shifting his weight from side to side, staring down at the floor. This had been the sign, when he was little, that he was about to throw himself on the ground and scream. "Besides," he said, looking up, "I'm not the one that does drugs."

"Morgan, go to your room." Perry felt Karen's hand on his shoulder. "It's late and your father's tired."

"He's always tired. I wonder why that is."

"Don't be cute," she said.

"I'm not hungry," Perry announced. There was a shrill beeping from the microwave, but he didn't do anything about it. "Maybe you can get through to him. I can't talk to him when he's like this."

Perry went to the bedroom to lie down. There were raised voices in the kitchen, then yelling, then the slamming of the screen door. He turned and switched off the lamp.

"He says he's not coming back," Karen said when she came to bed. She sat upright in the dark, her hands folded in her lap.

"We've heard that before," Perry said. "Besides, he's got it too good here, and he knows he can't go back to Donna's." Morgan had lived with his mother since the divorce. But then Donna had remarried, to a buzz-cut engineer, a churchgoing man with a daughter in college and his own ideas about parenting. Things had gotten bad over there. Morgan had broken the rules, stolen money, sneaked out of the house. He would hide out for two, sometimes three days in a row before coming back. Eventually, Donna had given up. "We can't do this anymore," she'd said, "we won't. You have to take him." It had been a year of Morgan living in Perry's house, but he couldn't say things had gotten any better.

"He'll come back," he said. He reached out, grasped her fingers, and squeezed them gently.

Three months later, Morgan called to ask Karen for money. Then, for two years, they heard nothing.

Perry felt in his pocket for the note from the coroner's office. He took it out and unfolded it. There was a street address, but no city or state, no name or commentary. He called Charles and went downstairs to wait.

Perry had no real sense of the city's geography, but the address, Charles told him, was uptown. They drove up Magazine Street, a long corridor flanked by antique shops and antebellum houses. Fences of cast-iron enclosed gardens filled with broad-leaved banana trees, shrubs of blooming sweet olive, and stately magnolias, bare of flowers. The air, damp and sluggish, smelled like ripe peaches.

Perry got out at a pocket park across the street from a liquor store, then weaved through two lanes of traffic and stepped into a doorway. The door had been painted over several times, and wood grain showed through chips of blue, green, and purple. He pressed the button next to the mailbox, but no one answered. He remembered Morgan's keys and tried one in the lock. The latch turned, and the last key on the ring let him into the apartment at the top of the stairs. He called inside, then slipped into the front room and closed the door behind him.

Two tall windows faced the park, the view obscured by gauzy curtains and half-open shutters. The front room was filled with rippling shadows, as if the building, maybe the whole world, were underwater. He flipped the switch at the wall, brightening the strings of Christmas lights tacked along the moldings. There was a shabby opulence to the place. The leopard-print couch, missing a foot, had been propped up on a stack of library books. A black rotary phone was on display, and next to that a turntable and a stack of old records. There was no television.

The photos on the walls were dark and glossy. In one, a naked man with a hairless chest perched on a carpet of upturned nails. In another, a snarling woman held a cigar stub in one opera-gloved hand and a mug of beer in the other. He stopped at the third and stared. Beneath the dunce cap, the tramp's five o'clock shadow, and the grease-paint smile, he still recognized the boy. It was Morgan.

Behind him, the door opened with the sound of a jingling collar. A muscular dog trotted into the room and squinted at him. It lifted its tail, lowered its flat head, and barked. At the other end of the leash was a tall white woman in a tank top, her head crowned with a tight nest of dreadlocks. She was small-breasted and braless, with blond tufts thrusting out from the hollows below her arms.

"These pictures," he blurted, "this one, I mean—" He felt in his pocket for the note but couldn't find it. "Sorry, I was looking for Morgan."

"Get out." The dog let out a trio of barks, then stood there panting. The woman loosened her grip on the leash. "Right the fuck now." Perry sniffed and wiped his nose on his sleeve. He hadn't noticed it dripping before.

"No, I'm not a—I'm Perry, Morgan's dad. Wait, I have ID." He began to reach for his wallet, but the dog's eyes were on him. The animal stiffened, and Perry froze.

"How did you get in here?"

"The coroner. There were keys to this place, when they gave me his things. You must have—does he live here?" The dog strained against the leash. "Irma," the woman said sternly, "sit." She crouched to the animal's level and soothed it. "Look, she's very protective. Wait outside, all right—I'll be down in a minute." She moved away from the doorway, leading the dog along the edge of the room. Perry did as he was told.

He got as far as the curb before he had to stop and retch. The back of his throat convulsed three times, the last so hard it bent him over. He spat froth onto the sidewalk. He hadn't thought this through. He knew that now. It must have been ten years—no, more than that—since he'd gone a day without pills, not since his back surgery.

The front door swung open and the woman stepped outside. Her dreads were covered by a crocheted hat and she was snapping together the last buttons of a cowboy shirt.

"Are you okay?"

"I'm fine, just getting over a cold."

"Well, keys or not, you shouldn't go into somebody's house like that. You could get hurt." She rummaged in her purse and retrieved a crumpled pack of cigarettes. "You're as bad as Morgan, you know that?" He wiped his face with his shirtfront. "A babe in the woods." She lit one, tossed the lighter back in her purse, and held out her hand. "I'm Geneva."

"Perry." She had a firm grip and the skin of her hands was rough and dry.

"You're from Chicago, too?"

"Chicago? No, Des Moines."

"I knew it, that little liar." She smiled for the first time, and tiny lines appeared at the corners of her mouth. She'd seemed younger at first, but now he placed her age somewhere between thirty and thirty-five.

"You have my keys." He handed them over and watched as Geneva locked the door. What business did she have with a nineteen-year-old boy? He knew it was crude, but he felt proud. He liked the idea that his son had been laying a grown woman. Not some girl bewildered by her own desires, but a woman who could choose for herself. The cars started moving, and a breeze, hot and gentle, skimmed the length of the street. Over the tang of exhaust, he caught her scent—a perfume of aniseed and day-old sweat.

"You know he didn't live here, right," she said, turning back. "Not really."

"No, I guess I didn't."

"Mostly he stayed at the Twat Mahal." She pulled a cell phone out of a front pocket of her jeans. "Shit, I'm late. Walk with me, okay?" He followed, lengthening his stride to keep up. "So about a year ago, the Nobodies found this big empty warehouse in the Ninth Ward. They've been squatting there ever since. It's fucking foul. Honestly, it smells like a sewer."

"I don't understand. The who?"

"The Nobodies Zirkus. They're these kids that put on shows around here—some classic circus stuff but mostly, I don't know what you'd call it, just gross-out nastiness. They were on tour for a while, but the van broke down, so now they're back again."

A tremor passed over his face. He wasn't crying—hadn't been able to cry—but his eyes began to water. "And Morgan, he was one of them?"

"Not exactly. He was part of that scene, yeah. But sometimes, you know, he would just get sick of all of them or they would get sick of him and he'd need somewhere to crash."

"And you would let him stay with you. The two of you were close."

She shrugged. "I don't know about that."

It came on at once—surges of sweat, his skull filling with a damp thumping. He was dying, he was sure of it, his whole body putrefying and pooling into his shoes. He put one hand on a parked car and vomited into the gutter.

"Come on," Geneva said, taking his arm.

She pulled him through a door and into a blast of air-conditioning. A murk of cold smoke swirled above the concrete floor. There were voices and laughter, the crack of billiard balls and the senseless chiming of gambling machines. She helped him onto a stool, and then there was ice water in front of him and an old-fashioned glass filled with whiskey and cola. He gulped down the water and shivered.

"Sorry," he said. "I don't think I'm used to the heat."

"Like I said, I'm late for my shift." She put her hand on his shoulder. "I'm sorry about what happened to Morgan, really. A lot of people are. I mean, he was a sweet kid." She produced a pen and flattened a napkin on the bar. "Some of us are having a thing for him tonight at this place on Saint Claude. You should come. You know, if you feel up to it." He put one hand on the bar to steady himself.

"Wait," he said, turning to catch her arm. But she was already gone.

Back in the hotel, he texted Karen. "Everything is fine," he told her. "Morgan is coming home," he said. "I will be back tomorrow." And finally, "Sorry." He knew he should have said something before he left, tried to explain that this trip was something he had to do without her help. But that conversation, they'd have to talk about so many other things, and he wasn't ready for that.

He turned the AC as high as it would go, shut down the phone, and tried to sleep. The muscles in his legs tingled and twitched, as if an electric current were running through them. He kicked off the comforter first, then the bedsheets, then lay on his back, squirming. He thought about ordering room service, but the idea of food made him nauseous.

He sat up in the bed and tried to clear his head, to push away the noise and numbness long enough for something to move inside him. He knew he owed Morgan a father's grief—and hadn't that been the point of doing without the pills, of coming here in the first place? But it was like trying to tune in a broadcast on an old television: faint images and the sharp edges of voices muffled by a shroud of white noise.

He rummaged through his store of memories, grasping for one with the power to stir up the right kind of feelings: holding Morgan in the hospital, birthday parties, camping trips, working together in the shop.

None of it worked. It all turned so quickly into a version of pity for himself. The poor, sick man who'd lost his son.

It was still light outside his window. He closed the shades, took the comforter off the bed, and wrapped it around his shoulders. Seated on the thin carpet, he turned on the television and waited.

It was nine-thirty when Charles picked him up at the hotel. They turned off Canal and onto Rampart Street, keeping the French Quarter at their right. Three forms, like clouds of chalk dust, burst in front of the headlights—children in white T-shirts darting through a darkened crosswalk. Charles stopped the car, but he didn't reach for the horn.

The bar was little more than a brick shack with an iron gate for a door. Neon signs for Pabst and Abita glowed behind its black-barred windows. He stepped onto the corner and handed Charles the fare. On the sidewalk, rows of blue and white tiles spelled out MARIGNY and ST. CLAUDE AVE.

"I'm not trying to scare you or anything, but you know this isn't Bourbon Street, right?" Perry nodded. "Looking for a midnight stroll, I'd pick another block, ya hear me?" Charles reached out the window and patted Perry's arm.

It was dark under the low ceiling, and on his way to the bar, he tripped over a footrest from a broken recliner. A fan in the corner pushed the air around, but it didn't help the smell. A film of stale beer and locker-room funk stuck to the surface of everything. A sign, hand-written on a scrap of cardboard, leaned against the shelf of liquor bottles: THIS IS THE 8TH WARD. NO FROU FROU DRINKS.

He ordered a beer and waited for Geneva. Balanced on a stool, he swung his feet above the floor, trying to shake the sting out of his legs. His eyes had stopped watering, thank God, but yawning, that was his latest affliction. The woman behind the bar set a bottle in front of him. "Don't go to sleep on us, now." She smiled sweetly, revealing a row of rotten teeth.

The man who occupied the stool next to him looked barely out of his teens. He was husky, with a wisp of beard that ran from jowls to chin. He wore a thin button-up, translucent with sweat, and a cheap sport coat, the near shoulder torn and showing stuffing. The brim of his bowler hat was low over his eyes, and he had a stick pen, mangled at one end from persistent gnawing, which he used to scribble into a sketchbook.

"Sorry," Perry said, "but is there some kind of event here tonight, for Morgan Eastwood? He was hit by a car the night before last."

"Moron?"

"What?"

"Numbskull Moron. The kid that got hit on the bridge. Skinny, right, big eyes, curly hair?"

"His name was Morgan. Did you know him?"

"I saw him around." The man looked up from his drawing, and for the first time Perry saw the tattoos—a harlequin pattern, black blocks above his eyebrows and red daggers stabbing down his cheeks. "Hold on, you're not a cop, are you?"

"No, nothing like that. I'm his dad."

"Oh, sure. Right on." The man scratched under his hat with his pen. "I wasn't trying to be an asshole. That was his name. His clown name." He pointed to the corners of his mouth and grimaced. "Get it? Like Buster or Pipsqueak. He was Numbskull." A woman in thick-soled boots and a dress of soiled taffeta approached the bar. She wiggled her hips, tugged up the drooping bodice, then threw her arms around the back of the clown's neck. Forgotten, Perry went back to his beer.

It was at least an hour waiting, so he switched to whiskey. It wasn't what he really wanted, so he figured it shouldn't count against him. The place had been empty when he arrived, but now the booths and the thrift store furniture, along with most of the floor space, were occupied by sweating bodies. White bodies, for the most part. Something he wouldn't have noticed in Des Moines. But he'd been told New Orleans was a Black city, and these people, they didn't look like tourists. Where had they all come from?

The burning in his legs worsened, and suddenly he had to scramble to the toilet. When he stepped out, it was darker than before and a bare light shone down on the back of the room.

"We were on Chartres by the old packing plant," a voice said over the PA. "And there were these two dogs that hung around there, a black one and a little white one. They were both wild and mean as hell. So I saw them on the corner there, and I said to Numbskull, 'Let's see if we can get them to chase us.'" Perry stopped pushing his way to the bar and turned around. There was no stage, and the crowd kept him from getting a good look. "So Numbskull takes off, pedaling like crazy—he charges them, laughing his head off."

Others came to the front to offer stories and tributes: Morgan had been a freeloader and a liar, but he'd also built bikes and given them away, shared his tools, and taught anyone who wanted to learn how to make repairs. He would take falls, even hurt himself, if he thought it would make someone laugh. Once, on a ferryboat, he'd saved a friend from drowning, kept the boy from slipping over a guardrail and into the Mississippi.

When Perry got back to the bar, he found that a girl had taken his place. Her bare freckled arms were folded across her belly. She seemed to have been crying, and when she turned to look at him, he saw innocence in her rough-hewn face, its wet eyes and wide mouth.

"Are you really his dad?" she asked.

He nodded, and the girl got up from her stool. She hugged him and planted a sloppy kiss on his cheek. "I'm sorry," she said.

He took his seat, humbled. These strangers, they had probably seen Morgan more clearly, maybe even loved him better, than his own parents. The truth was, Perry had left the family long before Morgan ran away. He'd had so little left to offer at the end, hardly more than room and board and knowledge of a trade. Morgan had needed something else, and maybe he'd been right, no matter how it all turned out, to go off on his own.

When he saw Geneva, she was in the middle of things with an expensive-looking camera, snapping pictures of a girl in a fur hat.

"You look like shit," she said when she found him at the bar.

"Must be the flu."

Her forehead tightened. "You don't have to lie."

"One of those twenty-four-hour things," he continued. He looked down at his drink and pushed the ice around with a straw. "Must have been the plane. All those people."

"Have it your way." When the bartender brought her drink, Perry insisted on paying.

"I meant to ask—Geneva, what kind of name is that?"

"It's Gen," she said. "Genevieve, actually. Geneva's a kind of nickname. With these kids, there's all this drama. But I'm neutral. I'm Switzerland."

"So they're your friends, then."

"Some of them. They're my subjects, really. It's not the same thing." She fixed a new lens to her camera and stepped away from the bar. "We'll be ready to go soon, but I need to take a few more." He yawned again and, not worrying what anyone thought anymore, laid his head in the crook of his arm and closed his eyes.

"Come on," Geneva said, waking him. She set a wad of bills on the bar. "The ghost bike's here."

Outside, a caravan was gathering, kids like the ones inside, drinking beer and smoking weed on the corner, mounting their salvaged bikes or guiding them in aimless circles in front of the bar. Their machines were simple and worn out, layered with rust and cracked paint. Some had wire baskets in front where bottles of beer, full ones and empties, rolled around and chinked together. The owners had improvised repairs: a seat stay lashed to the crossbar with bungee cords; a butter knife jammed between handlebars and basket to stop it rattling; a saddle like a gutted mattress, the exposed springs and torn vinyl bandaged with duct tape.

One rider sat astride two bicycles fused together. The handlebars and seat of the bottom frame had been amputated, and another frame, stripped of its wheels, grafted onto the stumps. The rider, a shirtless man draped with a black feather boa, was perched at the top, a crow on a clockwork roost.

Geneva pointed to a bike that was lashed to the rack with a length of chain. It was a sturdy, unlovely thing, a one-speed with back-brakes and thick balloon tires. He took it for a child's bike at first, except that it was saddled so high and white all over, slathered with house paint so that even the spokes and the gears were the same shade of raw cotton.

"It's about two miles from here," she said. "The bridge where it happened." She fit a key into the padlock. "Amanda was going to ride it, but now that you're here, she wants you to do it. Can you ride?"

Sick as he was, he'd have to try. His bike back home, a composite fork locked to an aluminum frame, Tiagra shifters and a Shimano wheel set, had been sitting unused in the basement for years now. He used to take it out on country roads on the weekends. He'd grip the drop bars, curl his body into a taut "S," and work through the gears. It had curved beautifully, responding to his weight, yielding just the right amount without tipping over, like a dancer when she's being dipped. It wasn't that he'd forgotten, but those memories were from a different life, the one before. Before the back spasms, before the surgery and the scripts for Percocet and Oxycontin, the need to keep them coming.

He shuffled forward, swung one stiff leg over the frame, and settled onto the saddle. He'd failed Morgan in so many ways, but he could at least do this. He had to. A few off-color notes from a trumpet and the beating of a bucket drum announced the start of the procession. He got the ghost bike up to speed. Wherever it had come from, the thing had been left outside a long time. Water had gotten inside and rusted out the bearings, causing it to pull from one side to the other. Turning was clumsy, and he nearly tumbled into the street as they rounded the corner from Marigny onto Rampart. He knew he should be thinking about Morgan, but with the fire searing his legs, he could hardly think at all.

There were few streetlights and what moonlight there was seemed to get tangled up in the mess of wires that sagged from the utility poles. Narrow, single-story cottages lined the street, a patina of dust muting the bright colors of their clapboards.

Shivering in the dank heat, he struggled to keep up with the pack.

Geneva had an ornament, like an onion cast in silver, hooked to the underside of her seat. He tried to keep it in sight, assuring himself that she wouldn't leave him behind. One hand pushing on the top of a thigh to keep it moving, he limped through an intersection. Four cats, collarless and lean, lay panting in the middle of the cross street. He hunched over the handlebars and pushed into an open space.

Crossing rows of railroad tracks, his wheel caught in a gap and pitched him onto the grit of the railyard. His hands and arms stung where little rocks had cut them, but it didn't feel like a serious fall. Still, he didn't want to stand. He began to cry, then stopped. It was only for himself, of course. He couldn't cry for Morgan, probably didn't deserve to. Nearby, an iron rail reflected the dim orange of sodium light. He wondered how long it would take for a train to come along and finish what he'd started.

Then Geneva's hands were on his arms, her shoulder under his, lifting him to his feet. Eyes stinging, he swayed on legs gone nearly numb. He was glad it was her, that she'd been the one to find him in the dark. He placed his hand at her hip and stumbled forward. Pressing his face against her hair, he drew in the sweet stink of her.

"Knock it off," she said, pushing him away. Geneva brought the ghost bike to where he was standing. Gently, she steadied him and helped him to climb onto the seat. When was the last time someone had helped him onto a bicycle? It must have been when he was little, his father.

"You can do it," she said. "It's not far now."

His awareness contracted, transforming the street into a narrow tunnel. There was only the pedaling and the pain in his legs now, the heat and the stinging blur of sweat dripping into his eyes. When they turned back onto a major street, he looked up. There was a rusted bridge ahead, spanning the width of a shipping canal. By the time he reached it, he'd given up any hope for redemption. *This is what being haunted is*, he thought. *It's owing a debt to the dead and not being able to pay it.*

At the bridge, he leaned the bike against the guardrail, looped a chain around it three or four times, then hooked the lock through one of the links. He snapped it shut. The girl from the bar, the one who'd been crying, took the key from his hand and threw it in the direction of the river. A cheer went up and one of the circus people held out a torch. There was the smell of butane and then the roar of flame unfurling itself. Perry stood very still and looked into the eye of a camera, watching as it snapped open and shut, fixing the harsh truth of him.

Creek People

STAN'S SISTER would never admit it, but she didn't have near enough money or strength left to keep up that house by herself. There were small things: doors that stuck, a water heater that left red-brown puddles on the basement floor, a split flue tile in the chimney. The foundation, cracked at the corners and still settling, was probably the worst of it. And then there was the roof. She'd had it patched in places, but rain and melting snow still leaked through the asphalt, spreading dark stains on the undersides of the eaves. The last big storm, Sandy had hauled buckets of rainwater through the living room and down the stairs, then dumped them out in the basement drain, where the neighbors wouldn't see.

All that, and she still wouldn't hear of letting it go. Never mind that the rest of the neighborhood thought their family was trash, or that Stan was the only pair of hands left to help her. Never mind that on an afternoon like this, the first and probably the last mild Saturday of a long sweltering June, when he should've been in his backyard in a lawn chair with a beer in his hand—or better yet, making love to his wife with the windows open—it was Stan, and not Sandy's ex-husband or her grown boys, who was out back, down on his hands and knees, scrubbing and sanding the deck.

It was hours scouring the boards before the job was done. When the planks were clean and smooth, he fetched a broom from the kitchen. He was sweeping away the sawdust when he heard something metal, a ring, ticking against the sliding door. Sandy scowled at him through the glass.

He couldn't get over how old she was looking these days, how much like their mother. There were crow's feet at the corners of her eyes, and flat, brown spots were edging out the freckles that ran along her arms and shoulders. To save money, she'd taken to setting her hair with a kit from the supermarket. Her perm was thin and porous; it radiated from her scalp like a halo of dishwater foam.

He turned away, but the next second she was out there with him, breathing down his neck.

"Jesus, Stan, were you just going to sweep it all into the yard?"

She took the broom, handed him a dustpan, and started to move around the deck, gathering the powder into neat little piles. It had been like this since they were kids, Sandy telling him what to do and then how to do it.

There were a couple of wrought iron chairs in the yard, and he thought about how much he'd like to hurl one at the house, put it right through the glass door. But that would cost him too much. Sandy had his job, his house, his whole life in her back pocket. He bent down and held the scoop while she whisked the last of the mess into the pan.

"I have to run some errands. Can you set out some beef to defrost?"

"Sure," he said without inflection and went into the house.

At the bottom of the stairs, he snatched at a dangling cord until a bare lightbulb glared down on the deep freezer. The inside still had a wispy coat of frost, but it breathed out a raw stink. He didn't hear the motor buzzing, and when he put his hands inside, he found thawing meat leaking juice all over the bags of vegetables and the softening dinner rolls.

He went to the stairs and called up for Sandy, but she didn't answer.

"Sandy, goddammit, it's the freezer!"

Nothing.

He went back to the freezer and dragged it far enough away from the wall to squeeze in behind. It was plugged in, and he couldn't see anything wrong with the cord, so he tried the other outlet. The icebox shuddered once, then started humming.

He got out from behind and assessed the damage. Anything he thought could be salvaged, fruit mostly, he took upstairs, washed in the sink, and packed into the refrigerator. He stuffed the meat into a couple of doubled-up Hefty bags, sealed up the freezer as best he could, and pushed it to the stairs. It wasn't as heavy as he thought, but the sound of the blood and water sloshing around inside made him queasy. He dragged it up the stairs and out of the house. In the yard, he turned the thing sideways and sprayed it out with the hose.

By the time he was done, the sky had turned shades of purple, and his back throbbed in time with the crickets. He went inside and settled his weight onto the couch in the living room. Sandy's husband had left seven years ago, but the room was the same, as if she were a custodian, looking after it until the real owner came back. The walls were painted forest green and hung with paintings of outdoor scenes: wolves and winter landscapes, a flush of mallards startled into flight. Richard had taken his six-pound bucketmouth from over the fireplace, but the bare hooks were still anchored to the studs.

During the divorce, Sandy had been so stubborn about the house, so unmovable, that Stan couldn't help admiring her a little. The sensible thing would have been to let Richard have his way and sell the place, then stick it to him in the settlement and move back to the valley. She could have had a few easy years that way, living off the alimony.

But leaving that house on the hill would mean she couldn't walk around with her nose in the air anymore. She'd have to go back to being a Hubbard, a low-town cricker. So she chained herself to that big empty house and let Richard and his lawyers walk away with everything else worth taking.

He heard noises from another room and when he went to investigate, he found Sandy in the kitchen. Her purse was on the floor, and she was standing in front of the refrigerator with the door open.

"What happened here?"

"Freezer went out. You've got a bad outlet down there."

"Damn it." She opened the freezer door and shifted things around. "Where's the rest of it? The steaks, at least."

He shrugged. "It must have been out since the other day."

"Damn it," she said again, and closed everything up. With her head cocked and one hand on her hip, she looked at him like he was a dog that had just taken a shit on her carpet. "What about the deck, you didn't get the sealant on?"

"No, Sandy, I was a little busy lugging your freezer around."

She sighed and shook her head. "Well, it couldn't take more than an hour, could it? If we get started now we can put on a first coat at least."

He went to the sink and started washing up. "It'll keep. Besides, I told Mel I'd be home for dinner."

"Call her, then," she said, brightening. "We'll make something here. It'll be a family dinner. Oh, and she can stop by the store. I mean, it doesn't look like there's much left here." This too was somehow his fault. "I'll make her a list," she said, and tore a sheet off the pad stuck to the refrigerator.

His jaw tightened. "You ever think maybe I don't want to spend every night over here, that maybe it's not my purpose in life to be your step and fetch it?"

"Don't be nasty."

He dried his hands, and when he crossed the hall to the bathroom, she followed him. "I'm going home," he said, searching through the cabinet until he found the Tylenol. He tossed a couple in his mouth and then scooped in water from the faucet.

Home. That was a joke. For two years, he'd been living in his dead mother's house. Before that he'd been in Kansas City, broke and out of work. Sandy had found him a job in Hopsville and given him Mom's house to live in. He'd hated the idea, but it was a rope dropped down a dark hole, a way out of the mess he'd made of his life, and he'd grabbed for it. She'd done right by him at the time, and he was grateful. But that was two years ago, and this was now.

"All right," she said. "We'll just have to get an early start tomorrow."

"What do you mean?"

"Well, we can't leave the deck like that—what if it rains? And you need to mow the yard. You know you've been putting it off."

"Mow it yourself."

Sandy leaned across the narrow doorway. It was clear she wasn't going anywhere, so he shoved past her into the hall.

"And while you're at it," he said, "why don't you drag that freezer back to the basement? You could fix the outlet while you're down there." He opened the front door and left it open. "I've got news for you, Sis—I'm not your handyman, and my wife isn't your goddamn maid."

At home, he parked the hatchback in the garage, set his toolbox back on the shelf, and went inside. Melina stood over the stove, stirring ground beef into a sizzling mash of olives, raisins, and boiled eggs. He took a slow breath through his nose and held it, savoring the scent of simmering wine until cayenne tickled his lungs.

His mother's house had never smelled this good. A childhood of instant mashed potatoes and dry, gray-white pork chops hadn't prepared him for Melina's cooking: for slow-grilled short ribs bathed in chimichurri sauce, for cumin-spiced meat pies filled with red peppers, for sweetbread and chitlins.

Melina had thickened in the handful of years since the wedding, but he didn't mind. He took a moment to admire the way her sundress clung to the shape of her hips, then put his arm around her waist and nuzzled her.

"So, how is Mr. Foster doing? Did he try to dance with you again?"

"The poor man," she said, turning off the burner. "Some days he thinks I'm his wife. If no one looked after him, he would spend the whole day in dirty pajamas and never put his teeth in." Stan got a beer and sat down at the faded Formica table. Melina got plates from the cabinet and started setting their places. "How are things at Sandy's?"

He shook his head, then got up from the table. "I don't want to talk about it."

"Another fight?"

"It's nothing. I need to take a shower."

After dinner, he settled into the recliner, the one his mother had slept in most nights near the end, and graded the last of the summer-school papers. Melina opened the doors to the mahogany cabinet that held the old console television and the record player. She flipped through the channels before settling on the usual sitcoms.

When he couldn't bear to read another confused essay about the Declaration of Emancipation or the Compromise of 1777, Stan joined her on the couch. *The Dirty Dozen* was on cable. He tried to get her to watch it through to the end, but she fell asleep somewhere in the middle, during the assault on the château.

What did Sandy see in that house, anyway? It had been out of place to begin with, and though the neighbors wouldn't say it to her face, they still held a grudge. Widow Best had lived quietly on that spot for seventy years. But then some bad wiring had shot off a spray of sparks in the den, and flames had scorched her grand Victorian to the foundation stones.

That was tragedy enough, but Richard and Sandy had done the unthinkable. Without consulting anyone, they had swept in, bought the lot, and raised a modern split-level in the midst of the all those gingerbread manses. As far as the rest of the neighborhood was concerned, the place should have never been built. It was a scandal from base to boards.

Besides, everyone knew that Richard Gooch had married down. Most families on the hill were the descendants of Hopsville's founders, gentleman farmers who'd left Kentucky for Missouri. The rest were heirs to the bankers and factory bosses who, not long after, had bought the town outright. Stan's sister was the only exception. Her people had been the cast-offs from neighboring counties—penniless latecomers who had set up shanties at the edge of Hog Creek, toiled in the shoe factory, and caused trouble in town. Later generations hadn't done much to improve the family's reputation.

Their father, Frank Hubbard, had been one of the worst. A hard drinker who liked to fight, he'd spent more than a few nights in jail. At home he was moody and free with his fists. As a boy, Stan had put his body in the way of it, tried to keep the old man off his mother and Sandy. When he showed up to school with bruises or a black eye, the whole town knew who was responsible. Sandy could put on airs, but she was Frank Hubbard's daughter, and the Hubbards would always be creek people.

Melina stirred, and they both got ready for bed. She changed into her nightgown and stood in front of the bathroom mirror. Watching her like that, as she brushed her teeth and spat into the sink, he could almost forget about Sandy and the house, about the suffocating feeling he got whenever he pictured the rest of his life pinned to this speck on the map, his future tangled up in its meager history.

He thought about the way Melina kissed him, like there was still something in him that she needed to go on living. He thought about how, after they made love, she would sometimes swing one leg across his hip and wiggle her ass with happiness. Just now, waiting for her to come to bed, he could breathe again.

The next day, a sound like an angry dog jolted him awake. Nine-thirty in the morning and Bill Tender was roaring down the street on that ridiculous crotch rocket.

Stan got dressed, put on some coffee, and sat down at the kitchen table with the *Hopsville Dispatch*. There was an ad in the classifieds for an apartment in the low part of town: clean, two-bedroom, not far from the Food Barn. If Sandy was smart, she'd put the house on the market today and get herself a place like that.

When Melina came back from Sunday Mass, they ate lunch together. Afterward, she traded the simple dress and rosary for a bikini and a trashy novel and lay sunning herself in the backyard. Stan had a little fun menacing her with the hose then went around front to wash the car.

He was waiting for the wax to haze when the phone started to ring. He didn't move to answer it.

"If it's Sandy, I'm not here."

Through the kitchen window, he watched Melina pick up the receiver and turn away. He was moving the shammy in wide loops across the hood when the screen door slammed. Melina stood on the front porch with no towel or robe to cover her, giving the whole neighborhood a good look.

"What's with you?"

"It's Sandy. She was mowing the yard."

"That's a first"

"There was an accident."

They went inside, and he lifted the phone off the counter. There was a voice on the line, but he couldn't understand what it was saying or why the words were making him dizzy. He had to ask for it all again.

The mower had taken the tips of three toes, the voice told him, on Sandy's right foot. She had lost some blood, was shaken up, of course, but was going to be fine. He hung up the phone and put his hands on the counter to stop them shaking. He wasn't going to feel sorry for her, a grown woman who couldn't mow her own yard and didn't want to learn.

A little unsteady, he went over to the recliner in the living room. He took the paper from the side table and unfolded it. Melina rushed to the front door and dug in her purse for the car keys.

"What are you doing?"

"Nothing." He tried to read, but he couldn't put the words together.

"Your sister is in the hospital," she said, as if there might be some misunderstanding. "We have to leave."

"I'm not going over there. Think about it, me kneeling at her bedside—'Oh, poor Sandy, please forgive me.'" He pulled out the sports section and unfolded it, rattling the paper to emphasize his point. "It's just what she wants."

"It's not a trick, Stan. She's in the emergency room."

"They said she's stable. That means she's going to be fine. Look, you don't know her like I do. Three toes to have the last word, to make sure I know who's boss? A bargain at twice the price."

He looked down at the paper, focusing on a photo from ringside: one fighter on his back, the other man lording it over him, daring him to come back for more.

"*Sos un forro,*" Melina said. She left the house and made a big show of slamming the door behind her.

The rest of the afternoon, he sat on the back porch with a cooler of Budweiser. At first he felt guilty about not going with her, but after the third or fourth beer he was able to forget about it. Across the alley and days ahead of the holiday, the Tender kids were launching screamers out of coke bottles, two or three at a time. The little rockets whistled over the roof, then ran out of breath and blew themselves apart.

Stan loved the Fourth of July. When he was a boy, the whole family had gotten up before dawn. His mother served flapjacks with maple syrup for the kids, pork chops and scrambled eggs for their father and Uncle Jimmy. The men, still drunk from the night before, drank mugs of black coffee then headed into the woods with fishing rods and tackle.

As soon as the sun was up, Stan would burst outside with the paper bag from the fireworks stand. He set up Folgers cans on the fence posts, dropped in sizzling cherry bombs, then dashed to cover before the blast launched them into a neighbor's lot. Mom sat on the trailer steps with her cache of Winstons. She stared out at the road and lit each new cigarette with the glowing stub of the last one. Sandy and Stan lit Black Cats and strings of Lady Fingers, and when Mom went inside to fix lunch, they stole off to the toolshed, took down a hammer, and burst the unexploded ones against the concrete.

In the evening, Dad would shimmy out of the pickup truck, a bag of ice over each shoulder, and Jimmy, still whistling "Yankee Doodle," would set a pine barrel on some patch of level ground. Mom would go inside to fetch the milk and sugar while Dad smashed up the ice to mix with rock salt. Jimmy would set Sandy on top of the churn, and Stan would work the crank, mashing it all together with walnuts and strawberries from the garden. Before Melina came along, those had probably been the happiest days of his life.

He was dozing in the recliner when he heard the garage door open. The streetlight on the corner was buzzing, and for a solid minute he couldn't tell if it was night or early morning. He brushed sandwich crumbs from his shirtfront and took the empty plate into the kitchen.

Melina was sitting alone at the table sulking over a platter of cold cuts; she had a paring knife in her hand and was using it to cut thin slices from a wedge of Chubut. He put the plate in the sink. When he pulled out a chair, it made a scraping noise against the tile.

"So," he said, half sitting, half falling into the chair, "how is she?"

"You're drunk."

It was hot, and he could feel his hair, thick and damp, against his forehead. He raised his hand to untangle it, but then thought better of it; that would only make him look guilty.

"A few beers," he said, and scratched the back of his neck. Something behind him started twittering, then launched into a full-throated shriek. He turned around, expecting to see—he didn't know what, maybe a starling drowning in the sink.

Melina took the kettle off the stove. She poured herself a cup of tea and stood at the counter. He could see now that she had been crying.

"What are the doctors saying?"

"Another surgery tomorrow," she said. "A specialist from St. Louis. They say he's a friend of Richard's."

Sandy would like that. It meant she could still play the doctor's wife. "The toes. They'll be able to save them?"

"Yes, they think so. But walking will be hard for her. It will take time."

"La invalido, huh?" He tried to sound good-natured, as if the whole incident had been a practical joke. He got up from the table and touched her arm. "Don't let her fool you. Sandy's tough as leather. Oh, she'll gimp it up for a few weeks all right, see what she can get out of it, but believe me, she'll be up and around in no time."

Melina took a sip of her tea, then set the mug on the counter and walked out of the kitchen. He followed her into the bedroom. "What? I'm sorry, okay, I shouldn't have made you go by yourself."

"You're her brother, you're supposed to help her."

"Help her? Jesus. What have I been doing for two years now? Cleaning out her gutters, hauling ass up a ladder—"

"Stop this," she said. "You have to stop." She took a deep breath and when she looked at him, her eyes, her face, every part of her was still.

The next day, Melina called off work, and they went up to Sandy's place. When they reached the old lane that formed the northern boundary of the town square, the hum of concrete gave way to the regular thumping of red bricks. It was almost Independence Day, and ranks of cellophane pinwheels had sprouted in the lawn behind City Hall. They twirled above the sod in shimmering circles.

"She's selling that house," he said. "I'm not spending the next twenty years holding up the walls."

At the bottom of the hill, he glanced at the marquee for Kaleidoscope Video. In black plastic letters, the owner had spelled out: SAVE A HOME. SHOOT A BANKER. As they climbed the hill, the houses of Hopsville's best families paraded by, the railings of their wrap-around porches draped with star-spangled fans.

"You sound like her, you know."

"What do you mean?"

"A martyr." She was smiling slightly, but mostly she looked tired. "Saint Stanley."

"What's that supposed to mean?"

"We chose to live here, to be a family."

"No," he said, shaking his head. "We didn't have a choice."

He'd put twenty years between himself and Hopsville, all but six of them in Kansas City. An honest-to-God city, with bronze statues and fountains. A Major League team. Shopping malls and freeways. But he'd ruined everything.

He'd been teaching at Westport, the shittiest school in the district. It was a place with metal detectors but no air-conditioning, where the students regularly called him a "motherfucker" and a "faggot." The bastards had torn the radio out of his car and taken a razor blade to the office chair he'd brought from home. Once, one of the older boys had tried to push him down a stairwell. He'd managed to tolerate it somehow, holding in his rage just long enough to get to the teacher's lounge or the parking lot.

Then there was the day when one of the little thugs, fresh from an out-of-school suspension, strutted into the wrong class. He took a seat in the back and started shooting the shit with his friends.

Wouldn't leave, wouldn't shut up.

His back to the class, Stan drew a timeline of the Russian Revolution, grinding the chalk so hard that it splintered.

The class erupted into laughter. He turned too late to see what had caused it, but that little bastard in the last row was grinning smugly, arms folded across his chest. Stan left the board and stalked to the back of the room.

"I told you," he said, "get the hell out of here."

"Go fuck yourself."

A sharp sound, like a book slapping the floor. Stan's hand throbbed, three of his fingers numb. It wasn't until blood spurted from the boy's nose that he realized what he'd done.

Even with the teacher shortage, no school in the city would hire him after that.

He said it again, this time just to himself. *We didn't have a choice.*

Out back, there was no sign of the freezer, but the old mower was there, overturned in a patch of rough grass. He tilted it right side up and unscrewed the gas cap. Gasoline sloshed inside, shimmering where the sun hit it. He replaced the cap and pumped the button a few times to push fuel into the line.

He cut the perimeter first, carving a pattern of straight, clean lines through the yard. The old mower didn't have a catch, and it spat clippings that stuck to the sweat of his ankles. Halfway through, he peeled off his soaked T-shirt and threw it over the deck railing. It hung there like a soiled flag of surrender.

When the job was done, he shut off the mower and wheeled it into the garage. In the laundry room, he rummaged through a hamper until he found a bath towel. He rubbed it quickly across his wet scalp, then snapped through a rolling rack of Richard's old island shirts. He picked one and tugged it off the hanger. It was tight in the shoulders and patterned with hula girls, but he buttoned it up anyway.

The carpet in the living room was tracked with fresh vacuum marks, but a pattern of dark splotches marked a path from the sliding door to the coffee table. He imagined Sandy crawling into the house, groping for the cordless, and then slumping over the arm of the couch to wait on the ambulance driver. Picturing her hurt like that and all alone, it made him want to be angry at somebody. He would have been, too, if he could just settle on who it should be.

As he stepped into the hall, Melina came down the stairs, an overnight bag slung over her shoulder. She'd been good with him that morning, better than he deserved.

"That shirt," she said, cupping a hand over her smile. "Where did you find it?"

"In the garage." He grinned and stuffed the tails into his jeans. "From the museum of Dick."

"We should go. The doctors will be putting her down soon."

"Under," he said. "They'll be putting her under."

When they got to the driveway, he started up the car. But then he just sat there, staring at the house. It had made him so angry, thinking about everything, that he hadn't put the car in gear.

"Stan?"

"She had no business keeping this place."

"Stan," Melina said again, placing her hand on his leg.

"No business at all."

At the hospital, they waited at the front desk behind a delivery man. The back of his neck was the color of a beefsteak tomato, and he smelled faintly of fertilizer. The nurse behind the counter signed and returned his clipboard. When Stan and Melina stepped up to the line of yellow tape, she still seemed to be admiring the white-washed basket filled with sunflowers and blue daisies.

"We're here to see Sandy Hubbard."

"Gooch," Melina corrected. "Sandy Gooch. They moved her this morning." The nurse reached for the basket.

"These just came for her." The desk phone rang and she answered it. Propping the receiver to her ear with one shoulder, she flipped through the pages of a binder. "407," she said, not looking up. "And would you mind taking these? You're going already."

"407," Stan repeated. He lifted the basket off the counter and followed Melina to the elevator. When they got to the room, Sandy was lying in bed with her eyes closed and her mouth open. Stan set the basket on the ledge under the television, and Melina approached the bed.

"Sandy, it's Melina and Stan. Are you awake?" Sandy blinked and rolled her head on the pillow.

"Look who decided to show his face."

Melina gestured toward the basket. "Someone sent you flowers, Sandy."

"Oh," she murmured, propping herself on one elbow. "Who are they from?"

Stan slipped the card from under the bow.

"A lot of people, I guess." He read four or five of the names before he realized what they had in common. "The school board."

"That's nice. Some people know how to act." She smiled and eased back against the pillow. The same look as at Mom's funeral, her and Melina half-concealed behind a wreath of red and white carnations. They'd made the deal right then, he was sure of it. Sandy would give up her share of Mom's house on Flood Street. She would throw her weight around with the superintendent, open up a spot for Stan at the high school. But it would be up to Melina to talk him into it, to convince him to give up on Kansas City. To fetch him home for good.

"Does it hurt?" he asked.

"Like the devil, but what do you care?"

"We should go now," Melina said, "and let you rest."

The bedsheets covered Sandy's feet, the bandaged one a shapeless bulge. It was strange to imagine the carefully painted tips of her toes underneath, now purple or black, the cut ones at least. He pictured them sewn back to the stumps with a crooked ring of stitches, like she was the Bride of Frankenstein.

"I almost forgot," Sandy said. "I told the Campbells they could use the ice cream maker."

"The one Uncle Jimmy used to bring around?" He pulled aside the flimsy curtain and looked down on the parking lot. "What do they want with it?"

"It's for their little ones, for the holiday. Don't you remember?" she said. "It was every Fourth when we were kids."

"Thing's an antique," he said. "Probably rusted out."

"Look at Mom's place for me, see if it's there."

"*Our place*. That's what you meant to say." He turned away from the window, ready to start something, but Melina's look asked him to let it go. "I haven't seen it," he said.

"You haven't looked." Sandy gazed down at her hands and smoothed wrinkles out of the hospital blanket. "Just leave it in the garage the next time you're over to my house. Brenda will be by for it."

"Brenda Ross? The one who started everyone calling you 'shit cricker' in the cafeteria?"

"It's Campbell. It's been Campbell for twenty-five years now—what's wrong with you?"

He fidgeted with the flowers, plucking pastel spears off the daisies. They don't have enough of their own, he was about to say, they have to help themselves to what's ours? But just then one of the nurses breezed in, a flat-chested girl in a blue smock.

"How are you feeling, Mrs. Gooch?" She moved about the room with a casual efficiency, checking the monitors and the IV. "We need to get her ready for surgery now. You can see her after."

"We brought some of your things," Melina said, crouching to set the bag on the floor. "I'm going to leave them right here."

She raised up, ready to leave, but Sandy caught her by the wrist.

"Don't let him forget. You know how to talk to him."

By the time it was all over, the sun was nearly down. On the drive home, he imitated Sandy's voice, the husky jangle of it, like shaking a sack of broken glass. "You know how to talk to him." Melina hid her eyes behind a pair of sunglasses and leaned back against the headrest. He waited for her to show some sign of support or say anything, really. But she just sat there.

"The two of you," he said. "You're in it together."

"Fine." She made gestures in the air, as if she were casting a spell. "We made a witches' bargain. Cursed you with a job and a place to live, washed your clothes and cooked your meals."

"I think we both know Sandy never made a meal worth eating." He forced a little laugh, but Melina ignored him. "Look, you've seen how it is. In St. Louis or Kansas City, nobody cares if your uncle couldn't pay his debts or your granddad got hammered in the middle of the day. But around here? It's sins of the father for seven generations."

"We have sins of our own."

"Oh, give it a rest, will you?" He shifted in his seat and put his hand over hers. "Sure, we did some sneaking around at the start, but the way he treated you, that pig, he'd given up any right to call you his wife."

"Not that," she said, drawing her hand away. "You were lucky to get a job. Any job. After what you did."

His body gave a jerk, like taking a shot of bourbon. They'd talked about it before—what to do, what he would say if lawyers got involved, reasons, even, for how it happened, what had gotten into him. But this was different. She was saying he was a bad man, that he ought to be ashamed of himself.

Something started to rise up in him. It made him feel small and fearful and it was going to swallow him up if he didn't do something about it.

"It must be nice to have a clear conscience," he said. He pulled up to a stop sign, took one hand off the wheel, and crossed himself. "How about I do ten Hail Marys, and you can bathe me in the blood of the lamb and we'll call it a day."

"*Que disparate.*" She looked away, shaking her head. "Pull in there," she said, pointing to the lot in front of the Always Save. "We need some things from the store."

He pulled up to the curb, but before he could cut the engine, she was stepping out of the car. Leaning out the window, he called after her. "So, what, you're walking back?"

She showed him the back of her hand and then the automatic doors closed behind her and she was gone.

Once he was home, he tried to forget about the argument. He knew if he thought about it too much his chest would start to burn, and juices from his stomach, tepid and sour, would rise to clog his throat. He started in on a documentary about the Civil War, then thought about going down to the basement. He'd seen the ice cream maker down there a few days ago behind a box of old photographs.

He went out to the driveway, lifted the car's back door, and folded down the seats. If Sandy really wanted that old junk, she could have it. He'd drive to her place, let himself into the garage, and leave a heap of it next to the mower, right in the spot where Richard used to park the Lincoln. He loaded Mom's TV first, wedging it in with boxes from the basement. Three trips and the car was packed full. He settled the ice cream maker into the passenger side and got in.

Not wanting to cross paths with Melina, he took the back way to the hill. He skirted the edge of the railyard, crossed the tracks, then passed through the factory's shadow. As he approached the one-lane bridge over Hog Creek, a shape moved at the edge of his headlights. He laid off the gas and a woman—no, a girl—came into focus. Headphones over her ears, she was ambling beside the guardrail, deaf to the world.

Scare some sense into her, he thought, and blew his horn as he passed. The girl in his rearview was standing in a band of streetlight, shouting after him, punching the air with her middle fingers. His teeth ground together, and sweat stung his forehead like an insect he wanted to swat. He hit the brakes hard, but then just gripped the wheel and let the engine idle. He'd left the girl a few yards back, but she was closing the distance.

She should have been frightened, alone after dark with an angry man. She should have turned away and run home. He'd teach her a lesson, goddammit, show her what she should've learned already: that a man was a thing to be scared of.

He unlatched his seat belt and stepped out onto the bridge. He was trembling, thrilled and frightened at the same time. Something was going to happen now, he was sure. He didn't know if he'd be able to stop it or if he wanted to.

"Hey," the girl shouted, "asshole!"

The tendons in his neck went taut.

"What the hell was that? You think—" She stopped, then went bashful. "Oh God," she said, stuffing her hands in the pockets of her denim jacket. "Mr. Hubbard. Jesus, I didn't know it was you."

He stood there blinking at her. There was a tinny throb coming out of the little speakers in her ears, a sound like a car that wouldn't start. The ground beneath him wobbled, and he had to put his hand on the back window to steady himself.

"Mr. Hubbard?"

Why had he gotten out of the car? Why had he stopped in the first place? His hand slid along the hatch until he was sitting on the bumper.

"Are you okay?" The girl crouched next to him, her tangled hair glowing in the brake lights.

He made a noise like a hiccup or a muffled sob. Maybe Melina was right; maybe he wasn't a good man after all.

"Mr. Hubbard?"

He drew one arm across his eyes, sniffed hard, and tried to shake it off. "You're Jay Lobe's girl, aren't you?"

The teachers' lounge had filled him in on the Lobe girl long before she showed up in his homeroom. A year older and a head shorter than the other girls in her grade, she'd made her reputation early. She'd tackled Betsy DeLaney in the lunch room and yanked a fistful of blond hair from the girl's scalp before the monitors could break it up.

"What are you doing out here?" he asked, mostly to buy some time. The world had begun to right itself, but his breath was still coming shallow and short.

"My dad's pissed," she said. "It's nothing, just a bad night."

He'd grown up with Jay Lobe. A mean, snub-nosed bully who'd only gotten worse with age. No question, any daughter of Jay's had seen her share of bad nights. He didn't feel like yelling at this girl anymore, or scaring her, or whatever it was he thought he was doing out there. There was no sense to it.

"You moving or something?"

"What?" he said, then remembered the pile of junk in the car. "No."

The Lobe girl looked to the far bank of the creek, as if there might be someone back there who could tell her how long she had to stand there or what she was supposed to do.

"You sure you're all right?"

He nodded. "I was just working today," he said, "in the yard. The heat." He reached out one hand and pushed against the bumper with the other. "Help me up, okay?" He fumbled in his pockets for his keys, then realized they were still in the ignition.

"Look," he said, "it's dark. Why don't I give you a lift? It doesn't have to be home."

She looked him over, his red face and his rough hands, then shook her head. "Thanks anyway," she said, putting her headphones over her ears once more. "I gotta go."

He watched her cross the bridge, her pace faster now, until she was out of the reach of his headlights. He walked once around the car, just to make sure he had his legs under him, then climbed inside. On his way to Sandy's house, he started to think about the Lobe girl's father and his own. But he didn't let it get too far. For years, he'd done his best not to think about the old man. That invited comparison, and he didn't like what they had in common.

He pulled into the driveway, lifted the garage door, and took the ice cream maker inside. He set the barrel and the crank on the bare floor, next to the mower. Back at the car, he opened up the hatch and sized up the load, trying to decide what to take in first: a stoneware jar from the days when the bachelor uncles let the hogs go hungry and fed corncobs and bails of barley to the still; an army parachute, dyed red for a blanket; a framed picture of a dead boy in a dapper suit, lost when his scarf snarled around a wagon's spinning axle. It seemed pointless to him now, and low, to leave all that junk for Sandy to come home to. The hatch made a solid sound when he closed it. He pulled down the garage door, leaving it open a crack for Brenda Campbell, and got back in the car.

There wasn't any starting over, not really. But maybe the Hubbard men didn't have to be bastards all the way down the line. He could give Melina a baby. There was probably time enough for that if they wanted it. They could still wring some good years out of this place. Halfway down the hill, he took his foot off the gas and coasted, letting the bulk of those old things bear him back into the valley.

The Watchman

THERE'S NOTHING much wrong with the Bridgeway Motor
Court. The carpet in Coleman's room is dappled with burn marks,
and the exterior wall, the one with the windows, has these psychedelic
zigzags at the bottom, like somebody's kid was left to run their cray-
ons back and forth over the same spot, rubbing them down to nubs.
It's cheap, though, the motel, and there aren't any bugs. Since his wife
kicked him out eight months ago, he's seen far worse.

At first, he'd spent nights at shelters or in the cab of his pickup, his
clothes and tools locked down in the covered bed. Then a space opened
up in a sober house downtown. The owner was a lawyer with connec-
tions in the probation department. He helped some of the guys with
their cases. Or gave them drugs. Especially the younger guys, the pretty

ones. I take care of you, you take care of me—that was his motto. Two weeks and Coleman was out of there.

For a little while, he was crashing with a buddy, a roofer with a spare room. The guy had this wallpaper in his bathroom, dogs playing poker. He must have thought it was funny, but every time Coleman went in there it made him gag, a furry paw to the back of his throat. Plus, he got tired of the bad nights: listening to the same stories over again, cleaning the guy's vomit off the toilet or the bathroom floor, putting him to bed.

So, the Bridgeway Motor Court.

In his room, he irons a pair of khakis and a polo shirt that says Apex Hardware on the front. He has a date tonight. On first dates, he likes to get there early, to be already seated in a booth if it's a restaurant. If it's a movie theater, he stands in the lobby, tickets in hand. He's been off the crutches since January, but there's still the limp. He doesn't like the idea of his date seeing him come through the front door half-lame, dragging one leg behind him.

He hasn't been dating long. Only four times since the separation, all through an app. Five if you count the one who stood him up. There was a college girl who'd left flirty comments on his pictures. They texted back and forth, and when it was time to meet, she made all the arrangements. He had never seen anyone walk like that—a rapid trot, self-consciously cute, as if her ankles were bound together by a short length of elastic cord. At the barbecue place, she'd ordered a lot of food and then, as he was taking care of the check, she asked the waiter to pack most of it up. He walked her to the MAX stop. She boarded the train carrying Styrofoam containers filled with pulled pork, hush puppies, and fried okra. He never heard from her again.

Then there was the wide-hipped woman with bleached bangs. They had dinner outside on the patio at Stormbrewer. The woman said, As a fat girl, it's kind of over the top for me to wear lipstick—like an unfair advantage. I have these big plump lips.

She smoked cigarette after cigarette, reapplying burgundy lipstick after each one, delighted by the red-painted filters as they piled up in the ashtray. She was funny and frank, and he liked her. In her profile, she'd said she was a social drinker. But while he sipped Coca-Cola, crunching on the ice with his teeth, she kept ordering whiskey sours, one after another.

You really don't drink? she asked.

I can't, he said. Not anymore.

Tonight, he is meeting his date at a diner, a Greek place that serves breakfast all day. In the display window a column of sliced meat turns slow circles. A song is playing, something about a laser in the night. He hasn't heard the song in thirty years, but then today, twice. He wonders if it's some kind of tribute, if maybe the singer has just died.

He orders a coffee and waits. The guy in the next booth is a loud talker; he asks the waitress where she's from.

Baltimore, she says and slides an omelet in front of him.

Did you like it there?

Hated it.

Nice train station, the guy says, as if that alone redeemed a place.

Coleman checks his wristwatch against the clock in the diner. He has to wind it often, or it runs slow. He spotted it one afternoon in a pawnshop window. It was silver colored, like the coin he'd gotten at his first meeting, his twenty-four-hour chip. The chip didn't mean much to him, but something about the watch—this ordinary, tarnished thing—it gave him chills. It seemed to be singing to him from behind the pawnbroker's glass.

My higher power, it can be anything? he asked at his next meeting.

Anything, they said.

The watch, then. Mine is the watch.

His date, Sandra, jangles through the front door and throws herself into his booth. Her hair is long and curly. Damp, it rests on her shoulders in thick, wet strands. She's breathing hard, like she just ran from somewhere.

I'm sorry I'm late, she says. It's my house, it's so haunted.

The waitress brings their menus. He already knows what he's getting (the baked lamb), but Sandra turns each of the laminated pages, squints at the pictures of food. A couple of her fingers look badly bruised. Smashed.

What happened there?

She sighs, regarding her hand. Do you believe in ghosts?

I'm not sure, maybe.

My house. Really, it's my sister's place. There's a ghost, maybe more than one. Like tonight. I was getting ready, and the thing slams a door on my hand. Bam!

Sandra slaps the table with the flat of her good hand. The silverware clatters, and the loudmouth in the next booth lets out a little shout— Ooo boy! Something like that.

Show me, he says.

Sandra holds up the injured hand. Between the first and second knuckle, her ring finger is purplish pink, darkening as it nears the tip. The pad is a shiny gray, almost black, as if it's been freshly inked.

Can you wiggle it?

The finger moves stiffly, and Sandra winces, waves it in the air.

I think it's broken, he says.

Are you sure?

Pretty sure. I used to work construction. New guys are always smashing their hands with hammers. That finger, that looks broken to me.

Shit, she says.

When the waitress comes to take their order, he asks for a bag of ice.

They eat dinner in the emergency-room waiting area. There are signs prohibiting smoking, but nothing about food. A man with a round florid face is giving them dirty looks, his hand over his belly, as if he's trying to keep his guts from spilling out. Coleman ignores him, goes back to sawing at his lamb with a plastic knife.

You probably think I'm crazy, Sandra says.

He chews, considering. I think you're hurt. I guess it doesn't really matter how it happened.

You've never seen a ghost, then—nobody in your family? The night my grandmother died, her ghost appeared in my sister Liz's bedroom. She was in bed with her husband. A Black man. Nana hadn't approved of the marriage, but that night she said she'd been wrong, that they had her blessing. Walter saw it too, said he'd never been so scared in his whole life.

Coleman hardly ever talks about the Watchman. But this, he figures, is a special circumstance. When I was a kid, he says finally, I was in a car accident. There was this man, he just showed up out of nowhere, and he saved me.

He'd been five years old at the time, playing outside, rolling over and over down the slope of his front yard. Grass stained his knees, and his hands stank of dandelion stalks.

He doesn't remember climbing into the family car, only the vinyl's sticky heat. On his knees in the front seat, he tapped on the faces of the dials, twisted the knobs, pulled the levers. The car creaked and began to move, drifting backward down the long driveway. Tires gnashed the gravel, and little rocks ticked beneath him. The yard, his house, they began to slip away. The way he remembers it, there were tracers, like the time he did LSD. The car was moving; so were the bushes by the roadside, the woods behind. All this moving, but Coleman couldn't move. It was like being in a dream.

He shut his eyes, and when he opened them again, he was not alone in the car. There was a man in the driver's seat, a watch loose on his wrist. Coleman tried to look at the man, but a bolt of sunlight flared off the watch's face and struck his eyes. The steering wheel jerked to one side, and the car veered into a ditch.

That's all he remembers before the hospital. They'd pulled three broken teeth from his jaw. New ones grew in to replace them. After the accident, he knew he would never die. At least not until he was very old. Something was looking out for him, shielding him from harm. He could do whatever he wanted.

That's amazing, Sandra says. And no one else saw him?

We were out in the sticks. There was nobody around.

Sandra sets the plastic bag from the diner onto a little table built into the row of chairs. The bag says THANK YOU THANK YOU THANK YOU, and what's left of the ice sloshes around inside.

She says, You can go if you want to. It was really sweet of you to take me, but I think it's going to be a while. With her good hand, she takes a couple of fries from the container in her lap. Bet this wasn't how you saw your Friday night going.

I've had worse, he says, grinning. How's the finger?

About the same. Aspirin isn't doing much good.

Sandra holds up the hand. Two of the fingers are bound together with medical tape from the first aid kit he keeps in his truck. The ring finger looks wider than the others; the palm has begun to swell.

A woman with a crying toddler sits down nearby. Setting the boy in her lap, she presses a damp cloth to his forehead. Sandra watches them, seeming—for the moment, at least—to forget about her injury.

Do you have any kids? It didn't say in your profile.

A daughter, he says. Heidi. She'll be five next month.

Does she . . .

She lives with her mom. We're separated. Almost a year now.

So, why did she leave you? Sandra asks.

He considers objecting. What does this woman think she knows about him? He couldn't have been the one to leave?

I was a drinker, he says.

Sandra picks absently at her food and tosses in the fork. She snaps the container shut and sets it at her feet. The boy has stopped crying. He squirms out of his mother's lap and totters around, his bare feet leaving outlines on the vinyl tile that wilt and then disappear.

Coleman looks away. It is hard for him to be around young children. He doesn't even like to see them on television. His shame, it comes over him sudden and black, like someone yanking a sack over his head. The mother fills out paperwork, looks down at the clipboard, and then over at the boy. Sandra catches her eye and smiles.

I love kids, she says. I can't have them, though. Or maybe I could, but it would have to be somebody else's eggs. And who would that be? Not my sister, that's for sure. Anyway, I wanted to be a teacher, like for little kids, but then I failed out of early childhood education. Twice. I don't think they'll let me back in.

I work at a daycare now. When I first started, they gave me the hard kids. It was like—what do they call it?—hazing. There was this boy whose mother worked in a factory. We didn't open until five, but she'd be in the parking lot at four thirty, in the dark, her car engine rattling. We'd open early so she could make her first shift. She wouldn't come and get him until we closed at night.

That boy was so sleepy. First thing, I had to change his Pull-Ups. I'd show him the different ones and say: Hey, we gotta get up and save the world. Who are you going to be today? Iron Man? Captain America? He'd rub his eyes and pick an Avenger, and that's how I'd get him to wake up. These kids, you just have to treat them like humans.

Sandra, he thinks, is a good woman. But after they're through here and he's dropped her off back at the restaurant or her sister's house, that will be it. All this talk about kids, he wouldn't be able to take it. He wonders sometimes why he goes on these dates. Maybe it's because he wants to believe they're not true—the stories he tells about himself. He has two buckets for his life now: things he can't change, and things he can. The aloneness, it's stubborn, but he keeps pushing it back, hoping one day it will give.

So, Sandra asks, did you say you work construction?

Used to. Carpentry. I was a framer, mostly, but I did some finish work, too. That was before I got hurt. Busted up my leg, was on crutches for a while. Not much use on-site for a guy who can't get around. That's when I started at the hardware store. He pinches his polo shirt, puckering the fabric where the store name is stitched.

So they let you go? That really sucks. Were you hurt on the job?

Yeah, he says, lying.

It happened on a bright summer day. Alone in the house together, he and Heidi played Simon Says and danced the Hokey-Pokey. It was such a beautiful day, though—how could they waste it by staying inside? He got Heidi into her bathing suit and floats. He swept her up, put on her helmet, and strapped her into the child seat mounted to the back of his bike. He'd had a few pulls from the bottle in the basement, but he was definitely not drunk. He was just happy. They were going to the pool; such a beautiful day!

He pushed off the curb and started pedaling. Behind him Heidi was squealing, delighted. He wanted to do tricks. To pop a wheelie. Wouldn't it be funny? Wouldn't Heidi laugh? Just the idea, it made him laugh. It was all he could do not to laugh his head off.

He angled the handlebars, turning off their neighborhood streets and onto the avenue. They were going faster now, causing the wind to gust. But not fast enough for the car behind them. It swung out alongside, trying to pass. There was honking and the screeching of brakes and then a feeling like being hit with a baseball bat. His bike jerked out from under him and spun sideways in the air. A moment later, he slammed against the pavement, one leg tangled in the frame.

The leg was dead. He didn't look as he pulled it out of the wreckage. He got onto his good knee and crouched next to the red wailing bundle that was his daughter. He unstrapped her from the seat and pulled her close.

There was an ambulance. He let the paramedics examine her but kept a firm grip on the sole of her sneaker. Scrapes and bruises, they said, but she was going to be fine. It was a good thing she'd been wearing her helmet.

His daughter was all right and so he could feel again. Pain and anger. The driver who'd hit them was there, trying to apologize, to talk insurance. Coleman tore off his helmet and spiked it to the pavement. He raged. Tearful, he threatened to drag the man bloody through the streets.

A patrolman arrived to restore order, to take statements. All Coleman wanted was to get Heidi home, to go home himself, but the medics said the leg was fractured, that he needed to go to the hospital. And the patrolman, he kept asking his questions.

Sir, have you been drinking at all today?

The accident hadn't been his fault. But it was Coleman who blew a point-twelve on the breathalyzer, and it was his life, not the other guy's, that got ruined.

I know that store, Sandra says.

He's sweating now, and it feels like someone has put his leg in a vise.

Is it the one in Buckman? I had some keys made there a couple of weeks ago.

It's only temporary, he snaps.

All right, she says, okay.

He breathes in and out, takes a long sip of cold soda. He says, I'd like to start my own company. You know, down the road. Remodeling old houses, that sort of thing.

A male nurse wearing a blue smock and badge calls Sandra's name.

Will you be here when I get back? she asks, collecting her purse.

I'll be here.

He wipes the sweat from his face with a paper napkin. He curls into the narrow plastic chair, tries to get comfortable. He closes his eyes against the brightness of the waiting room, the television chatter, the noise of the sick boy, his shrill shouts of Mama! and No!

After a while his wrist begins to tingle. His hand, awkwardly bearing the weight of his head, has gone numb. He shakes blood back into his fingers and wipes the sleep out of his eyes, the groggy feeling of a nap gone bad. The ER is strangely still. The few people left in the waiting room are quiet, their heads pressed to their knees like the drawings on airplane safety cards. He is not sure if he's awake or dreaming, not sure if it matters.

He walks over to the automatic doors, and they open like fate. Outside, the parking lot is empty. It's nighttime, but harshly bright, as if illuminated by invisible floodlights. When he looks up, the stars are wrong.

It's only a few steps before the parking lot gives way to a forest. Gray trees, their trunks covered in pale mosses. There are birches, tall ones with bone-white boughs and smaller ones with branches that weep to the ground.

He walks for what seems like a long time. Past wounded trees, scarred by fire. It is so silent here. No birdsong. No chittering of squirrels. No rabbits rustling the underbrush, tracing frantic, crooked paths to their dens. Against his wrist, the watch gives off a fluttering heat, like something alive.

And then the forest is gone and he is standing in a clearing. A yard. A house. There is an old Buick parked in the driveway, a child bouncing in the passenger seat, playing with the knobs. Coleman starts walking toward the car, then runs. There's still time. If he hurries, maybe he can save the person inside.

ACKNOWLEDGMENTS

I'M INDEBTED to the Iowa Writers' Workshop for the teaching and support that I received there. Thank you, Connie Brothers, Sam Chang, Sasha Khmelnik, Deb West, and Jan Zenisek. Thanks also to my classmates, especially J. Daniel Duffy, Megan Freitag, Kirsten Johnson, Andy King, Melvin Lee, Amelia Maggio, Michaela Redcherries, and Gemma Sief. Thanks also to Katie Knoll and Jules Wood for sharing their passion for teaching and for their help with all things pedagogical.

Thanks to all the writing teachers, past and present, who've helped me with my fiction, especially: W. D. Blackmon, Ethan Canin, Charles D'Ambrosio, Tom Drury, Abi Jeni, James T. Jones, Daphne Kalotay, Margot Livesey, and Lindsay J. Mitchell. Thanks to Kevin Brockmeier for reading and commenting on the collection, to fellow writers Alana Franasiak and Brian Hauser for their insights and encouragement, and to Josh Gass for reading early drafts of so many of these stories.

Thank you to the editors and staffs of the following magazines and journals: Lisa Ampleman at *Cincinnati Review*, Chris Fink at *Beloit Fiction Journal*, Justin Jannise at *Gulf Coast*, Elizabeth McKenzie at *Chicago Quarterly Review*, Catherine Parnell at *Consequence Magazine*, and Evelyn Somers at *The Missouri Review*. These stories have been improved by their comments and suggestions.

Thanks to Abi Rupp for her friendship and for trusting me with a small part of her story. Thanks to the city of New Orleans and to

Shannon Brinkman, Ethan Clark, Nicholas Costarides, J. Dee Hill, Phil Hollenbeck, and Mary Richardson for lovingly documenting that city's beautiful bicycles and its subterranean scenes. I'm grateful to Ted Auch and C. D. Travenor for talking with me about hydraulic fracturing in Ohio. Thanks to Donna Dodson, Thomas E. Dodson, and Peggy Moots for preserving and sharing Dodson family lore. Thanks also to Jordan (stage name) at the Glitter Gulch in Las Vegas for speaking with me about strip club culture. I am also indebted to the work of a number of scholars, journalists, and memoirists—too many to mention—whose work I consulted while researching these stories. More about these sources can be found at https://thomasadodson.com/sources.

Thanks to the several bars, along with their staffs and patrons, that made their way in some form into these stories: the Deadwood Tavern in Iowa City, Charlie's Kitchen and Grendel's Den in Boston, and the Hi Ho Lounge in New Orleans.

Thanks to my family, especially my mother, for their love and encouragement. Thanks also to those who helped with my transition to Iowa City: Cate Campbell, Sam Cha, Russell Cox, Kate Estrop, Dawn Gabriel, Sue Kriegsman, Alana Kumbier, and David Taber. I am also grateful to the University of Iowa's Graduate College and Pam and Terry Hopper for their generous financial support as I completed this book.

This book would not exist without the hard work and expertise of the team at the University of Iowa Press. I would especially like to thank Amy Benfer, Karen Copp, Danielle Johnson, James McCoy, Allison Means, Susan Hill Newton, and Margaret Yapp. And finally, I'd like to humbly thank the contest judge, Gish Jen, for selecting the manuscript.

THE IOWA SHORT FICTION AWARD AND THE JOHN SIMMONS SHORT FICTION AWARD WINNERS, 1970–2023

Lee Abbott
Wet Places at Noon

Cara Blue Adams
You Never Get It Back

Donald Anderson
Fire Road

Dianne Benedict
Shiny Objects

A. J. Bermudez
*Stories No One Hopes Are
about Them*

Marie-Helene Bertino
Safe as Houses

Will Boast
Power Ballads

David Borofka
Hints of His Mortality

Robert Boswell
Dancing in the Movies

Mark Brazaitis
*The River of Lost Voices:
Stories from Guatemala*

Jack Cady
The Burning and Other Stories

Pat Carr
The Women in the Mirror

Kathryn Chetkovich
Friendly Fire

Cyrus Colter
The Beach Umbrella

Marian Crotty
What Counts as Love

Jennine Capó Crucet
How to Leave Hialeah

Jennifer S. Davis
Her Kind of Want

Janet Desaulniers
What You've Been Missing

Sharon Dilworth
The Long White

Susan M. Dodd
Old Wives' Tales

Thomas A. Dodson
No Use Pretending